True to the Wolf

True to the Wolf

Highland Shifters
Book 7

Caroline S. Hilliard

Copyright © 2023 by Cathrine T. Sletta (aka Caroline S. Hilliard)

All rights reserved.

This publication is the sole property of the author, and may not be reproduced, as a whole or in portions, without the express written permission of the author. This publication may not be stored in a retrieval system or uploaded for distribution to others. Thank you for respecting the amount of work that has gone into creating this book.

Produced in Norway.

This book is a work of fiction and the product of the author's imagination. Names, characters, organizations, locations, and events are either the product of the author's imagination or used fictitiously. Any resemblance to actual persons, living or dead, organizations, events or locations is purely coincidental.

ISBN: 979-8-3964-9655-2

Copy edited by Lia Fairchild

Cover design by Munch + Nano
Thank you for creating such a beautiful cover for my story.

CONTENTS

About this book	i
Chapter 1	1
Chapter 2	7
Chapter 3	14
Chapter 4	22
Chapter 5	27
Chapter 6	33
Chapter 7	37
Chapter 8	43
Chapter 9	48
Chapter 10	54
Chapter 11	58
Chapter 12	64
Chapter 13	71
Chapter 14	79
Chapter 15	85
Chapter 16	93
Chapter 17	100
Chapter 18	106
Chapter 19	113
Chapter 20	119

Chapter 21	125
Chapter 22	129
Chapter 23	136
Chapter 24	141
Chapter 25	145
Chapter 26	151
Chapter 27	157
Chapter 28	165
Chapter 29	172
Chapter 30	179
Chapter 31	187
Chapter 32	194
Chapter 33	201
Chapter 34	205
Chapter 35	213
Chapter 36	216
Chapter 37	223
Chapter 38	228
Chapter 39	233
Chapter 40	236
Chapter 41	244
Chapter 42	249
Chapter 43	254

Chapter 44	260
Chapter 45	266
Epilogue	269
Books by Caroline S. Hilliard	278
About the author	279

ABOUT THIS BOOK

Choosing anyone other than his true mate can destroy him. But a beautiful vampire might tempt him to ignore that.

Ever since he was a boy Henry has been determined to find his true mate, the one person who will accept him as he is and love him forever. Settling down with anyone other than his true mate has never tempted him. Until a beautiful vampire sends him to his knees.

The stunning woman has both his mind and body yearning for her, and if he doesn't find a way to prevent it, she might end up capturing his heart as well. But he knows giving in to his desire can only lead to disaster. Why then does it feel like his heart is ripped from his chest when she rejects him?

Eleanor can't give in to her feelings for the gorgeous wolf. Her sire would come after him and kill him. And she can't allow the destruction of the most amazing man she has ever met. To keep him safe she's left with only one choice—to leave him alone and let him think she doesn't want him.

But her stupid dead heart won't listen. And she soon finds herself following him under the pretense of protecting him from the evil witch who wants to kill them all. But will Eleanor be able to save him, or will she be the reason he dies?

This work is intended for mature audiences. It

contains explicit sexual situations and violence that some readers may find disturbing.

CHAPTER 1

Henry

Damn! Henry winced as he slowly turned his head to the side. His whole body was sore like he had been run over by a truck. Not that he knew what that felt like, but it must be similar to this.

He cracked an eye open and blinked a few times to focus, until he realized his vision wasn't the problem but the closeness of the wall that was facing him. It was just about touching the tip of his nose.

After pulling his head back, he focused on the tiled wall. Despite the darkness in the room, he could see just fine, but he could swear he had never seen that tiled wall before.

Henry turned his head to the other side and frowned when he stared straight into a shock of messy dark hair. Someone was lying next to him on the hard floor in what was clearly a bathroom.

The person's scent suddenly registered, and he

shuddered with a mixture of desire and trepidation when it filled his lungs. He recognized the scent. Eleanor's. But there was a tang to her scent that he didn't like. An unmistakable stench of charred flesh.

Pain sliced through his right arm when he sat up abruptly, but he was more concerned about Eleanor than his arm. Unless the vampire had just roasted a large animal on a spit, a smell like that wasn't a good sign.

After getting up on his knees, he reached out and turned the light on. They were in a small bathroom he had never been in before. But he had no idea why they were there or what time of day it was. There weren't any windows in the small room, so it was impossible to tell how long he had been out cold.

Frowning, he stared down at the beautiful woman on the floor. She was lying on her back with her head turned away from where he had been lying. Her pale skin was flawless with no indication of any burns that would explain the scent.

Henry gripped her chin and turned her head to face him. Her cheek that had been hidden from him was a little red, indicating a first-degree burn, but it wasn't nearly bad enough to give off a burnt smell.

Perhaps he had this all wrong, and they had been lying on the floor for quite a while. Any damage she had suffered from the sun or a fire was almost healed, and the stench might be just a trace lingering in the closed room.

Henry frowned as he studied Eleanor's relaxed features. What had happened to make her expose herself to the sun or a fire? It would have had to be something serious, or he couldn't imagine she would have risked it.

The last thing he remembered was lying on the bed next to her, right before dawn in the bedroom on the second floor of Hugh and Kynlee's farmhouse. Something had obviously happened after that to render him unconscious, but he had no recollection of what it was.

But whatever had happened, someone had moved him to this bathroom with Eleanor. Unless Eleanor was the one who had moved him. It might well have been her, since she had been the one closest to him.

An image flashed in his mind of a huge fire. The mansion owned by the panther clan just north of Fort William had exploded the night before. Bryson and Fia had left just a few minutes later to go back to Bryson's clan.

Henry turned his head and stared at the door. Were they still in the farmhouse? That had been his automatic assumption when he woke up, but perhaps he had been wrong.

Studying Eleanor's face, Henry debated what to do. Like the last time she had been sleeping or unconscious, he didn't really want to leave her. But she looked fine, and there might be someone else who needed him if something had happened to the house. There was no screaming to signal someone needed help, but he had no way of knowing without investigating.

On impulse, he leaned in and sniffed at Eleanor's neck, and his nose wrinkled at the scent of roasted flesh. After gripping her upper arm, he rolled her to her side to reveal her back.

"Oh, fucking hell." Swallowing hard, Henry stared

at her cracked, charred skin. The entire section of her back that he could see was nothing but a huge burn, and the T-shirt she was wearing had a huge hole with singed edges. Either she had been too close to a fire, or she had been standing with her back to the sun.

But how it had happened didn't really matter. The result was a horrible burn, and he didn't know whether she could recover from something like that or not. But he knew of one thing that might help. Blood.

After rolling her gently onto her back, he bit into his wrist until his blood flowed freely. Then he tipped her head back and pressed his wrist to her open mouth. *Please drink. Please drink.* He repeated the words like a mantra in his head while staring at her face.

He let his blood flow into her mouth until it started leaking from the corners of her lips, but nothing happened. She didn't swallow, and she didn't move. There was no response whatsoever.

"Eleanor!" Henry hissed her name as he pressed his wrist tighter against her mouth to stop the spillage. She needed every drop she could get to heal her back, and he would gladly give her everything he could until he was too weak to stay upright. If only she would take it.

He hissed for an entirely different reason when her teeth suddenly sank into his wrist. A spark of desire shot through his veins, but it wasn't nearly as intense as the last time her teeth had penetrated his skin.

Studying her face, Henry breathed a deep sigh of relief. "Thank God you're awake. Drink your fill, beautiful. I've got you."

Eleanor swallowed down big gulps of his blood without opening her eyes or responding to him in any other way. But the fact that she was drinking was enough. It had to mean that her back was healing.

Minutes went by, and he started to feel the weakness of blood loss. He should probably stop her before he grew too weak to do so, but he just couldn't bring himself to pull away from her after seeing the state of her back.

His muscles lost their strength, and he sank down onto his side on the floor. Blinking his eyes to focus, he kept his gaze on her moving throat. Her skin was rosy and healthy-looking, unlike the gray tinge that had been there before. His blood seemed to be helping.

"Henry." The sound of his name made him crack open an eye to see Eleanor staring down at him.

He must have dozed off because he couldn't remember her letting go of his wrist or getting up. Her eyes were wide and frightened, and he wanted to ask her what was wrong, but he couldn't get the words out. They were stuck in his dry throat.

"Did I attack you?" The fear in her eyes turned them a darker brown than usual.

Gathering his strength, he shook his head the best he could while resting the side of his head on the floor. He would have smiled to reassure her, but he simply didn't have the energy.

She nodded slowly but didn't look convinced. "Okay. But don't ever do that again." Her expression tightened, and she narrowed her eyes at him. "You should know better than to stuff your arm into the mouth of an injured vampire. I could've killed you."

Henry blinked slowly, trying to maintain focus on her beautiful face. She was right, but he didn't regret the choice he had made, and he wouldn't hesitate to repeat it if she was injured again.

"I have to get you some help, but the sun is up. Do you have a phone?" Her soft hand caressed his cheek.

Basking in her touch, he nodded weakly. His phone should still be in his pocket, unless he had lost it somewhere. And considering something had happened to them, it was of course a possibility. He still wondered what had made her brave the sun or forced her to endure an open fire, but his questions would have to wait until he was able to voice them.

Eleanor started patting him down, and he would have enjoyed it if he hadn't been so exhausted. It was an experience he would store in his mind to revisit later, even though she was only touching him to find his phone.

Henry wasn't as worried about his condition as the beautiful woman touching him seemed to be. As an alpha wolf it would take more than a little blood loss to kill him. Although he would need a few hours to heal before he was back to normal. But he wasn't able to tell her that.

She pulled his phone out of the front pocket of his jeans and held it up to his face to activate the face ID. "I know one of the people in the house is called Trevor. I hope he's okay. Do you have his phone number in here?"

Frowning, Henry nodded again. Her words confirmed that something had happened in or to the farmhouse, and she didn't know if the others were okay.

Apprehension tightened its hold on his mind, and he focused all his energy on voicing his question. "What...happened?"

CHAPTER 2

Henry

Eleanor's gaze snapped to his. "An explosion. Not the whole house. Most of it is still intact as far as I know. The corner we were in was completely destroyed, but the living room is on the other side of the house, so there's a good chance your friends are okay. I didn't have time to check, though. The sun was about to clear the horizon, and I had to find you."

Stunned, he stared at her.

Her gaze dipped to his phone as she swiped a finger over the screen, presumably to search for Trevor in Henry's list of contacts. Then she put his phone to her ear.

It seemed like his friends might be okay, and hopefully Trevor would answer his phone and confirm that.

But it was her last few words that had his mind spinning in shock. Was he the reason her back got burned to a crisp? That was what it had sounded like. She had risked her own life to find him and get him out of there. But why? Why would she do something like that for him?

"Henry. Thank fuck. Where are you?" Trevor's loud voice was filled with relief.

"This is Eleanor. We're in the bathroom in the barn. It seemed like the best place to take him after I dug him out of the rubble. He's weak but okay, I think." She studied Henry's face like she was looking for a sign that he wasn't.

I'm okay. He mouthed the words at her, but her expression didn't change.

"I'm on my way."

Eleanor lowered the phone, confirming that Trevor had cut the connection.

Only seconds went by before noise reached them through the bathroom door, and Eleanor quickly scurried into the corner of the room.

Henry had never been in the barn before, so he didn't know whether the sun could reach them if the door to the bathroom was opened. But he didn't have a voice to tell Trevor to stop. He would just have to trust Eleanor to know where to place herself to stay out of the sun.

The door was yanked open, and Trevor stared down at him. "There you are. How are you feeling?"

Nodding slowly, Henry tried to pull the corners of his mouth up into a smile, but judging by Trevor's frown, he wasn't very successful.

"I took too much. That's why he's so weak." Eleanor's voice sounded dejected.

Henry tried to look at her from where he was lying,

but she was outside his visual range.

"You should have known better." Trevor's gaze turned hard when it swung to the woman in the corner. "His arm looks broken. You should have let him heal instead of feeding from him when he was already hurt."

Henry shook his head where he was lying but Trevor wasn't looking in his direction. "No." The word was rough and barely recognizable, but it brought Trevor's gaze back to his, and Henry shook his head again.

Trevor's eyes narrowed into slits. "I'm not sure I can trust you and what you're saying, Henry. Not when I don't know what kind of influence she has over your mind."

Fuck! Henry was too weak to explain what had happened, but even if he could have, Trevor might not have believed him.

"I'm taking you back to the house and away from her." The large wolf alpha knelt beside Henry and scooped him up like he was a young child.

It usually took a lot for Henry to get angry, but the feeling of not being trusted and treated like a child had him fuming inside. "No." The word was still weak and didn't sound like the command he had intended.

Trevor paid no attention to Henry as he stormed out of the barn and headed toward the house.

Henry gathered all his strength to protest Trevor's high-handed behavior, but the words stuck in his throat when he saw the destruction to the house.

One corner was nothing but rubble, leaving a gaping hole into the rest of the structure. The remainder of the house was surprisingly undamaged, considering the complete obliteration of that one corner. And there was no sign of a fire. Henry had no idea what could cause that kind of destruction, except for the actions of one particular witch. Amber.

But why would she be content to take out just one corner of the house when she could have destroyed the whole thing? It seemed like an odd thing to do, unless she had been there for a very specific reason. To retrieve her mate, who had been located in a room close to the one Eleanor and Henry had been in.

Henry had about a million questions, but he couldn't voice them yet, and Trevor hadn't volunteered any information about the residents in the house and whether anyone was hurt or missing.

They entered the house through the front door and continued into the living room. After quickly scanning the room, Henry breathed a sigh of relief when he saw that everyone he knew was present.

Hugh, the panther alpha and clan leader, was standing with his arm around his mate, Kynlee. Leith, the legendary Loch Ness Monster, was sitting on the couch with his mermaid mate, Sabrina, in his arms. And Jennie, Trevor's mate, approached them as they moved into the room.

Gawen, Henry's most recent pack mate, turned to stare at him with his eyes widening in shock.

"He was in the barn with Eleanor." Trevor sounded irritated. "She almost drained him dry. But considering she was the one who called me, I don't think she intended to kill him."

Gawen took a step toward them. "Alpha?" Henry and Trevor were both wolf alphas, but Gawen's gaze was on Henry. "Do you remember what happened?"

Trevor sighed. "He's too weak to speak."

"I'm sure I can help him." Gawen pointed to an unoccupied couch. "Just put him over there, and I'll do what I can."

"Okay." Trevor strode over to the couch and laid Henry carefully down on his back.

Fia had told them how Gawen had healed her in the forest after she had taken a fatal hit by Amber's magic. But the man wasn't merely a witch. His power resembled that of a shifter but with a characteristic that Henry couldn't identify.

Gawen kneeled by Henry's side before giving him a small smile. "Just relax. This won't take long." Closing his eyes, the man put his hand on Henry's shoulder.

A strange sort of electricity shot through Henry's body and made him gasp. It wasn't exactly painful, but it wasn't pleasant either. The return of his energy felt magnificent, though.

It didn't take long before Gawen stood and gave Henry a short nod. "Do you feel better now?"

Henry laughed and sat up. "That would be an understatement. I've never had anyone heal me before. Is that how it always feels—like a burst of electricity racing through your veins?"

"I wouldn't know." Gawen shrugged. "It doesn't feel like that for me when I help someone, and I've never been healed by anyone else, so I don't know what that feels like."

"Does that mean you can heal yourself?" Sabrina cocked her head to the side as she stared at Gawen. "I didn't think witches could do that, or I guess warlocks in your case."

Gawen shook his head. "I'm not a warlock.

I'm...something else." The man's gaze dropped to the floor, and he frowned.

"Okay." Sabrina nodded slowly with a pensive expression on her face, but she didn't inquire as to what he was.

Henry wanted to know as well, and he had a feeling Gawen would tell him if he asked directly. But he wasn't going to ask in front of all these people when the man clearly wasn't comfortable telling Sabrina, who he already knew was a witch.

Besides, there were more pressing matters than knowing exactly what Gawen was. What had happened to the house for one. And then there was Eleanor.

The vampire had risked her own life to find Henry in the rubble, and instead of telling Trevor that it was Henry's own actions which had rendered him weak, she had made it sound like it was her fault. But before Henry went back to talk to her and make sure she was all right, he had questions.

He swung his gaze around the room until he met Leith's. "Do you know what caused the explosion?"

Leith frowned. "It was most likely Amber's work. Erwin is missing, and the room he was in is still intact except for a small hole in the wall. We have searched for him just to make sure, but the likelihood of him being buried is miniscule. Debris was pushed into the bedroom through the hole, which means he would not have been sucked out. Either he walked out on his own, which would be impossible in his state, or he was taken. And the person most likely to take him is Amber. That would also explain why she only destroyed a section of the house and not the whole structure. She was here to retrieve her mate, not kill him."

Henry nodded. "That sounds like a reasonable explanation. Anyone else hurt?"

"No." Hugh shook his head. "All in all, we were lucky. Only material damage, and that can be fixed."

"Good." Getting to his feet, Henry met Trevor's gaze. "I'm going to check on Eleanor."

Trevor opened his mouth to say something, but Henry held up his hand to stop him. "No, let me speak. I'm the one who stuck my wrist into her mouth to feed her after I saw the state of her back. She dug me out of the rubble out there even as the sun was coming up. I wasn't even sure she was going to make it when at first she didn't respond to me pouring blood into her mouth. But thankfully she did, and I'll be eternally grateful for what she did for me. So, don't blame her for me feeding her until I fell over with weakness. It was my choice, and she's already berated me for it, so don't you start as well."

Folding his arms across his chest, Trevor frowned. "And you're sure these are your memories and not something she put there to cover her ass?"

Henry gave a sharp nod. "Yes, I'm sure. And if you had seen the state of her back, you would've believed me. It was like charred meat. I've never seen anything like it on someone still alive. And I've never encountered anyone who would choose to do something like that to themselves to save another person who isn't a mate or loved one. She could've easily died."

CHAPTER 3

Eleanor

Eleanor stayed in the corner, even though the door was closed, and the sun couldn't reach her. She had an urge to go after Henry, an urge that was trying to overpower her instinct to stay out of the sun.

Taking a deep breath, she stared down at her fisted hands. What was it about Henry that pulled her like a moth to flame? It was almost like he had hypnotized her, but she knew he hadn't. She had been ready to die for him to make sure he was all right, and she had never done anything like that for anyone before.

Eleanor had helped people many times despite her maker forbidding selfless acts. The compulsion to follow her maker's command was strong, but it wasn't impossible to resist. Her sire was pure evil, and his maliciousness tainted her blood as well, but she still had her free will, even though it cost her to go against his expressed orders.

But risking her own life was another level of helping and not a very life-preserving one. At least not her life. She hadn't felt like she'd had a choice, though. Walking away without knowing where he was and in what condition just hadn't been an option.

After pushing to her feet, she went to stand in front of the mirror. "Holy hell." The woman staring back at her was a complete mess. Her curly hair was full of debris and sticking out in all directions, and her skin was covered in grime and dust. But at least there was a cure for that. She was in a bathroom after all.

Eleanor stripped out of her clothes before stepping into the shower. The water was cold at first, but it quickly heated to a soothing temperature, and she washed her hair and body to remove all traces of the explosion.

Smiling in contentment, she turned off the water and stepped out of the shower. It was strange how cleaning your body could have a cleansing effect on your mind.

A sound outside made her frown, and she snatched a towel from the rack next to the shower and wrapped it around her body. Someone had entered the room outside, but it was impossible to know who it was.

Henry's friends weren't happy with her at the moment, and one of them might be coming to tell her off, but she wasn't really worried about them. They might be angry with her for how she had treated their friend, but they were unlikely to hurt her, unless they considered her an immediate threat.

The door was yanked open, and she stared directly into Henry's worried hazel eyes. Words left her mind as she took in the glorious sight of his healthy glowing cheeks.

It was less than half an hour since she had taken most of his blood, but here he was, looking the epitome of strength and vitality. How, she had no idea, but it filled her with happiness to see him strong again.

"You're wet." His eyes widened, and his body tensed when he realized the double meaning of his words.

Eleanor snorted with laughter. It was impossible not to when faced with his cute awkwardness. Henry was quite possibly the least arrogant and flirty man she had ever met, and she liked that about him. He was the embodiment of kindness and respectfulness, but she had no doubt he would defend his friends and loved ones if necessary.

He was obviously attracted to her, but if anything it made him *less* forward and swaggering around her instead of more. Even though he didn't come across as a shy or weak man.

What she wouldn't give to rip his clothes off and fuck him until he exploded inside her. To feel his body jerk and see his eyes lose focus with pleasure would be amazing. She didn't even need to reach her own climax. Experiencing his and knowing she had given it to him would be satisfying all on its own.

"I'm sorry." He took a step back and started to close the door.

Hurrying forward, she reached out to stop the movement of the door. "Don't be, and please don't leave." Smiling up at him, she put a hand on his chest. "It's good to see you're so much better already. Were you faking it earlier, or did you just have a quick blood transfusion?" She winked at him.

"Seriously, though." Eleanor's expression sobered. "I'm really happy to see you're looking well. You don't have to tell me how you managed that so quickly if you don't want to. But I want you to know I'm sorry, and…"

She fisted the hand she had put on his chest and rapped her knuckles against his breastbone for emphasis. "*Promise* me you'll never do that again. No matter what. Unless I'm already dust, give me a cup of blood. Never your wrist or any other body part. It's too dangerous."

He stared at her for several seconds before saying anything. "I can't promise you that. But I'll take it into consideration if I have the time and opportunity to do so. Ultimately, it's my choice, though."

Crossing her arms over her chest, she narrowed her eyes at him. "And what do you think your friends will do to me if I cause you serious injury? Do you think they'll let me live?" It was a low blow since she didn't think they would kill her if she attacked due to starvation. She'd already attacked Fia once, and Bryson had let Eleanor live to see another night anyway.

Henry flinched, but his expression soon tightened into a scowl. "I'll make sure to tell them never to hurt you no matter what you do to me."

Eleanor sighed in frustration. It wasn't the response she had hoped for, but she wasn't surprised. Henry's kind heart trumped his own safety. "Well, I guess it doesn't matter. As soon as night falls, I'll be out of your hair for good. But it would've been nice to know that you've learned something from this and won't go sticking your wrist in any old vampire's mouth in the future. You'll end up getting yourself killed, and you're too good for that."

His lips tightened into a thin line, and he crossed his arms over his chest, mirroring her stance. "Have you considered helping us find and kill Amber? You already know her and have experienced firsthand what she's like. And we could use all the help we can get."

Eleanor wet her bottom lip while considering his proposition. She would have liked to help them, and she would have taken great pleasure in killing the bitch. But the risk was too high, considering who her maker was. Anyone associated with her was automatically at risk, because making friends was considered unacceptable behavior.

Shaking her head, she relaxed her features into a blank expression. "I'm sorry but I can't. I need to leave."

Henry's hazel eyes darkened as he stared at her. "Is there nothing I can do to persuade you to help us?"

She shook her head firmly again. "I'm afraid not. I can't help you."

Eleanor turned away from him before he could see the regret in our eyes. The urge to stay and make sure Henry remained safe was making her whole body tense. But she was used to resisting compulsions, so she would push through this urge as well.

"I'm sorry to hear that. I was hoping I could count on you, but I guess you have other more important responsibilities." The dejection in his voice was palpable, and even turned the other way, she could sense his shoulders slumping.

The image made her turn back to him, and she felt the urge to apologize for not being able to stay. But the words stuck in her throat when he took a step toward her with determination tensing his jaw.

His gaze dropped to her lips a second before he bent and covered them with his. Surprise and desire raced through her body, and she automatically parted her lips.

Henry's hand cupped the back of her head just as his tongue pushed into her mouth and twirled around hers, making her shudder with how much she wanted him. His kiss was hotter and more demanding than she had expected from a nice guy like him.

Pressing the front of her body against his, she eagerly responded to his kiss. But just as she was about to wrap her arms around his neck, he tore away from her and stormed off, leaving her gasping in his wake. The door to the suite slammed shut, and he was gone.

Several seconds went by before Eleanor could even move. If she still had a beating heart, it would have been slamming against her ribs hard enough to break her chest open.

"Henry." She whispered his name as she pressed her tight fists against her stomach. There was no reason for him to return to check on her again, and she couldn't go to him while the sun was shining. In fact, she didn't have any way to contact him at all. Which left her the whole day alone to think about how much she wanted him and how much she shouldn't.

Swallowing hard to push her feelings away, Eleanor let her eyes glide around the one-room guest suite. Someone had closed the blinds, shutting out the sun, and that someone had to be Henry. He had obviously done it before opening the bathroom door; she just hadn't noticed it earlier. It was yet more proof of his thoughtfulness.

And another reason he couldn't be hers. Henry was perfect for mating and fatherhood, but she could never give him that. Vampires could do a lot of things, but producing life wasn't one of them. And this was the first time she had regretted that fact.

Shaking her head to dislodge her train of thought, she stepped out of the bathroom and took a proper look around. It was a cozy room with a kitchenette in the corner and a large bed. It didn't have anything in the way of sustenance for her, but after drinking from Henry, she wouldn't need to feed for at least a day. And she would be gone before then.

Squeezing her eyes shut, Eleanor tipped her head back and took a deep breath. Vampires didn't really need to breathe, but she had trained herself many years ago to do so in the way a human would. And it had soon become second nature, like her body recalled being human.

Most vampires who wanted to blend in with human society breathed. But there were a few old ones who abhorred the idea of adopting human behavior. They considered it beneath them to assimilate lesser beings and would never do it. But they were typically the ones who didn't move in society much. Time seemed to take on a different meaning for those who were more than a thousand years old.

Eleanor wasn't nearly that old, though, but she was much older than Henry. If she was to take a guess, she would put him at around thirty, but it was hard to tell with shifters. He could be older but certainly nowhere near her own age. Just another reason to stay away from him.

She had been told she had a young mind, able to

keep up with the times and adapt without too much effort. But the older you were, the more baggage you carried, and that was true for her as well. And that was in addition to her evil and crazy sire, who would kill Henry on sight if he even suspected she had feelings for the gorgeous wolf.

Feelings. Eleanor used her fingers to gently untangle her curls while staring at the blinds protecting her from certain death. The pull she felt toward Henry was stronger than she had ever felt for anyone, and it wasn't all lust. Lust was definitely a part of it, but she would feel content just being near him. Or at least more content than she was at the moment. Her body was jittery, like someone had filled her veins with sparklers.

"Oh, for fuck's sake." She yanked the towel off her body and threw it onto the floor. "I can't let these stupid feelings rule me. I'm too old for that."

But to be able to overcome her infatuation with Henry, she would have to stay away from him. It didn't mean she couldn't work to ensure his safety, though, as long as no one understood what she was doing, and she didn't actually lay eyes on the man. And she knew exactly where to start. Locating Amber.

CHAPTER 4

Henry

Henry couldn't keep still. He had tried to sit down on the couch and relax while they were discussing what to do next, but it only lasted a couple of minutes before the tension in his muscles got too much, and he had to get up. Pacing to alleviate the discomfort, he tried to participate in the discussion, even though his thoughts were mostly centered around the beautiful wet woman currently stuck in the barn.

He had made the mistake of kissing her, something he would probably regret for days. The taste of her lingered on his tongue, and he caught himself gravitating toward the door repeatedly. What was it about her that was so enticing? Apart from her beauty, of course. He was affected by a beautiful smile just as much as the next guy, but his fascination with Eleanor ran deeper than that. Something about her called to him on a deeper level, making it impossible to think about much else.

"We'll be staying here to manage the repairs to the house." Hugh's brows were creased, and he had his arm tightly wrapped around his mate. "Our panthers need us to be present after what happened. This isn't the time for us to leave them alone to fend for themselves."

Leith nodded. "That is perfectly understandable. And we do not expect you to. However, I think it is time for the rest of us to regroup and decide on our next move."

"Yes." Hugh gave a sharp nod. "And I wish we could be of more help. But at the moment—"

"Don't worry about it." Trevor smiled. "Your place is with your clan, and we don't even know what our next move should be yet. Amber has retrieved her mate, but we have no idea what she'll do next or where she'll turn up."

"Well, at least there's no reason to expect her to come back here." Kynlee gave a small shaky smile. "If she wanted to kill us, she would've attempted it while she was here. We didn't even know she was around until the house blew up. But I guess it answered our question of whether she knew we had picked up Erwin."

Sabrina nodded slowly, her hand tightening on Leith's thigh. "Which begs the question *how* she knew. Amber met Eleanor yesterday, and that might've tipped her off. But how did she find Eleanor? How did she even know to look for the vampire that was supposed to be tied up in her cabin? I think Amber has the ability to locate people just like I have, except her ability seems to be more powerful and precise. It's the only explanation I can come up with for how she found Bryson and Eleanor so quickly. Because it wasn't coincidence."

"Unless she was here when we arrived back from the cabin with Eleanor and Erwin." Hugh frowned. "But is that even possible? She was seen with her daughter in Perth that day, but I'm not sure exactly when that was."

"I can check with Callum." Trevor pulled his phone out of his pocket. "But as far as I recall, Amber and her daughter were seen in Perth in the afternoon, and you weren't back here until well after dark. Amber would've had the time to get here before you arrived with her mate and the vampire."

Henry stopped pacing as a sudden thought struck him. If Amber had found Eleanor that easily before, there was nothing stopping the witch from finding her again. And judging by the way Bryson and Eleanor had been placed in the middle of the floor of that cottage, Eleanor would have turned to dust if Fia and Henry hadn't arrived early in the morning to prevent it. Whether Amber had intended for Eleanor to die or if it was just carelessness was impossible to say. But Henry wouldn't put it past the evil witch to have meant for the vampire to burn.

He was already by the door to the hallway before he realized what he was doing. Stopping, he locked his knees to prevent himself from going to her. Eleanor wanted to leave, and he had no right to stop her. No matter how much he wanted to protect her. It was her choice whether to stay or to go, and he had to respect that.

It was for the best anyway. Focusing on her would

only interfere with his search for his true mate. Not that he had actively searched for his mate yet. Taking over as alpha for a pack with issues had occupied all his time. But he had a feeling his infatuation with Eleanor would prevent him from seeing what might show up right in front of him. And the possibility of overlooking his true mate due to a temporary obsession was unacceptable.

He spun and looked at Leith. Henry had caught enough of the conversation around him to have a fair idea of the plan. "So, we're going to your house then?"

Leith raised his gaze to Henry and nodded. "Yes. We will meet the others there, except Bryson and Fia. I am not yet sure when they will be joining us, but I expect it will be late this afternoon or this evening."

Henry gave a short nod before turning and hurrying out of the room. He knew he shouldn't, but the urge to see Eleanor one last time before they left was too strong. She needed to know where they were heading. At least that was the excuse he was going with.

He had barely taken one step into the suite in the barn when he came to an abrupt stop. His jaw dropped, and he felt lightheaded as the blood flow to his brain changed course and headed south.

On the large bed lay a stunning woman, and her lips curved into a smile as she studied his face. She was on her back with her head and shoulders resting against a large pillow, her dark curly hair spread out around her head like a fan.

She was a vision, but what had made his jaw drop was the sight of her naked body. Her knees were bent, and her thighs were parted just enough to give him a clear view of her pink pussy.

His cock was hard as stone by the time he managed to rip his gaze away from her magnificent body. Fastening his gaze on a spot in the corner of the room, he cleared his throat. "You should…cover yourself."

Rage suddenly surged through him, and scowling, he closed the door behind him before staring into Eleanor's eyes. "It could have been anyone coming through that door, and you're completely exposed. What were you thinking?"

Her smile widened into a wicked grin as she sat up and leaned back on her hands. "I didn't expect visitors. It's not like I've got a lot of fans around here." She winked at him. "Except you maybe?" Her gaze dropped to his groin, and she licked her lips.

A shudder of pure lust rocked his body, and his rage evaporated as his gaze dropped back down to her pussy. *One taste. All I want is one taste.* It was a blatant lie, but he would run with it anyway.

CHAPTER 5

Henry

Eleanor was suddenly on her feet on the bed, towering over him and making him realize he had somehow made his way to the foot of the bed without noticing.

"Henry." Her arms wrapped around his neck, and she licked her lips again, drawing his gaze to her mouth. "If you're here to berate me, I want another kiss first."

He blinked at her. "Berate you? I was only—"

Soft lips pressed against his and cut off his words. And just like that his body took over. Wrapping his arms around her, he groaned at how good she felt against him.

The tip of her tongue licked against the seam of his lips, and he growled as he opened his mouth and rubbed his tongue along the length of hers before exploring every section of her mouth with eagerness. He was rough, but his control was shattered, and his desire was currently in command of his actions.

The sane part of his mind was telling him to stop and pull away, but every other part of him was telling him to take what Eleanor was offering and enjoy it.

She abruptly tore her mouth away from his, and he snarled with disappointment before opening his eyes to stare up into hers.

The mix of desire and sadness in her eyes made him pause and regain some of his control. "What's wrong?" His voice was rough, like he had just swallowed a pound of gravel.

"I'm sorry, Henry." Looking away, she let her arms fall to her sides. "I shouldn't have taunted you. It was wrong."

Narrowing his eyes at her, he tilted his head to the side to encourage her to meet his gaze. "I forgive you. Please look at me."

She bit her bottom lip before looking back at him. "You should let me go now."

"What if I would like to keep holding you, kissing you? I like you, Eleanor. The night we met, you told me we had amazing chemistry, and you were right. Don't you want us to explore that?" He should be looking for his true mate, but what if he never found her? What if this insane pull he felt toward Eleanor was the best thing he would ever experience? Was he willing to throw that away for the miniscule chance of finding his mate?

Her eyes widened before she squeezed them shut. "No, we can't. It's not…safe." The last word was whispered as her shoulders sagged.

"You mean Amber." He let his hand glide up her spine until it curved protectively around her neck.

"We'll take care of her. We have to. There's no other choice. So don't let the thought of her—"

"It's not Amber I'm worried about." Her eyes popped open. "Or I am, but she's not the only one."

Eleanor raised her hand and cupped his cheek. "My maker would kill you without hesitation if he found out we were spending time together. He abhors any feelings that aren't pure lust, greed, or maliciousness. Not to mention the fact that you're a shifter. By fucking you, I would be sentencing you to a painful death."

Henry was momentarily speechless. Her maker. He had no clue as to the typical relationship between a vampire and their maker. And it was one aspect of Eleanor's species he hadn't considered at all. Shifters were born not made, so he had no concept of what being turned meant in terms of control and obligation.

"Does he know where you are and what you do at all times?" He certainly hoped not. But Henry had been able to pinpoint Eleanor's location ever since she first drank from him. It wasn't a stretch to assume her maker had been able to do the same from the moment he turned her.

"No." She shook her head. "But he has a tendency to find out whenever I do something he doesn't approve of. And he doesn't bother to verify that he's got it right before he exacts punishment. He usually kills first and never asks questions later. No lives matter to him, except his own."

Henry's jaws were clamped so tightly his teeth were creaking in protest. It was on the tip of his tongue to offer to kill Eleanor's maker, and the only reason he didn't was that he didn't know what would happen to her if he did. Would Eleanor die if her maker was killed?

He took a deep breath to settle his simmering rage before he spoke. "What will happen to you if he's killed? You don't sound like you care about him." His gaze was locked on her face to judge her reaction to his question.

A small smile curved her lips, and she tilted her head to the side as she looked down into his eyes. "I hope you're not thinking of killing him for me. Because even though that's sweet, it would be a total suicide mission that I would never allow. Plenty of people have tried—powerful people. And he's been laying low since the last bunch thought they succeeded many years ago. But I think that's about to change."

He frowned. "What makes you say that?"

Eleanor sighed and let her hand drop to his shoulder. "He's started gathering followers again. But it's not your concern. You have enough on your plate at the moment. And the less you know about my sire the better. I don't want him to think he has a reason to kill you."

Henry lifted an eyebrow at her. "What will happen to you if he's killed? And I'd like an answer this time."

"Nothing." She chuckled. "Except I'd be deliriously happy to be rid of him. I won't wither and die if that's your concern."

He nodded once. "That's good to know." *And exactly what I wanted to hear.*

"Henry?" Trevor's voice sounded through the closed door to the suite.

Henry automatically tightened his hold on Eleanor and angled his body to shield her naked form from the entrance. "Don't open the door. What is it?"

"We're about to leave. Are you coming with us?" He could almost hear the frown in Trevor's voice.

"Yes, he is."

Eleanor's curt response slammed into Henry's chest and caused his eyes to widen in shock. "What? But—"

"No." She shook her head firmly with a determined expression on her face. "You're leaving with the others. And I'm leaving tonight after sunset." She put her hands on his arms and pushed them down until he had no choice but to let her go if he didn't want to hurt her.

Something tightened in his stomach as he stared up into her hard eyes. She had made her choice, and he would have to respect that if he didn't want to come across as an asshole, but he wanted to make sure she understood his position. "If this is just about you wanting to protect me from your maker, then I want you to understand that I'm not weak, and I'm not going to let someone like that dictate—"

"This is not just about my maker." Eleanor took a step back from him and crossed her arms under her chest.

His gaze automatically dropped to her breasts. Perfect handfuls tipped with pink nipples that he would love to tease until she begged for more.

He forced his gaze back up to hers. "Then what is it about?"

Her face was a blank mask, and her eyes lacked emotion when she answered. "You. I don't want you, so it's time for you to leave me alone. Please."

The meaning of her words pushed him back a couple of steps, leaving him to stare at her with his stomach twisting into a tight knot. Her words were spinning around in his mind with increasing speed, making him dizzy.

"Get out, Henry!" Her eyes were glowing red with anger when she yelled at him.

His head snapped back like she had just slapped him. But at least it brought him out of his motionless state.

He spun and stormed away from her, slamming the door to the suite behind him as he left.

Trevor and the others were standing by the cars when Henry hurried out of the barn. But he didn't meet any of their gazes before getting into the back seat of Trevor's car.

CHAPTER 6

Eleanor

Eleanor didn't know how long she had been staring at the door after Henry left. It might have been minutes or hours, and all the time she had been on her knees on the bed, shaking with a mix of rage and despair.

Rage because of what her maker would do to Henry if he ever found out she cared about the wolf, and despair because of how much she had hurt the sweetest and kindest man she had ever met.

Her cruel rejection of him had hurt him more than she had expected. She had anticipated disappointment and irritation, and perhaps even anger. But the pure pain in his eyes wasn't something she had expected. It had gutted her, and almost caused her to admit she was lying about not wanting him. Only the knowledge that she would be made to watch Henry being tortured and killed if her maker ever found out had stopped her from confessing she wanted him to stay.

"Oh, Henry." She buried her face in her hands as tears overflowed down her cheeks. "Be safe, my sweet wolf. Please be safe."

Eleanor let her tears flow while wallowing in the loss of someone special. She couldn't remember the last time she had cried, and she didn't think she had ever cried over a man before. But then she had never let herself feel anything for a man before. Unlike this time.

Henry had immediately caught her attention, and she had been powerless to resist him. Even as she had been running away after having been discovered in the kitchen with him by his friends, she had been plotting how to meet up with him again while making it seem like a coincidence.

But after her capture by Amber and the subsequent explosion, the thought of what her maker would do had made her decide to stay away from Henry. Except the wolf hadn't made it easy for her with his kindness and hot kisses. And the fact that she hadn't been able to resist taunting him hadn't helped either.

"Stop!" She swiped at the pink tears leaking from her eyes. "You're not a fucking baby. So, you'll suck it up and do what's necessary." And what was necessary was disposing of Amber and staying away from Henry.

Although, the evil bitch had proven to be more powerful than Eleanor had thought, and she had a tendency to show up when least expected. Eleanor would have to find a way around that if she was going to be able to kill the witch.

She still remembered how she had met Amber months ago. The witch had seemed like a nice enough woman when she approached Eleanor in an alley behind a pub. Eleanor had just finished taking a sip from a willing man who had been left thinking they had done something more sensual.

Amber watching Eleanor drink from the man must have alerted the woman to Eleanor's true nature, and the witch had seen it as an opportunity. After some negotiations, where Amber had demonstrated her grief over her daughter Mary's fate as a shifter's unwilling mate, Eleanor had agreed to give Mary her blood to try to break the mating bond.

Eleanor didn't think her blood would have any effect on the bond, but she had agreed to try anyway, swayed by Mary's seemingly hopeless situation. But instead of bringing Eleanor to meet Amber's daughter, the woman had taken Eleanor to her cabin. Once there the witch had taken over Eleanor's mind and rendered her powerless to the draining that had followed.

Her blood had been fed to Amber's mate, who was chained to the bed, and Amber had drunk some of it herself. But as Eleanor had expected, it had done nothing to break or reduce the strength of their mating bond.

After that everything grew hazy as she was left to starve. The days and nights blended and became one long stretch of dull pain as she slowly wasted away. Until Bryson, Fia, Hugh, and Kynlee arrived and finally ended her suffering.

Eleanor pulled in a deep breath and let herself fall back onto the bed. She was no longer in chains, but she felt just as restricted while she waited for night to fall. Until the sun set, all she could do was wait, and it was grating on her nerves. She needed to do something to get her mind off Henry and the pain in his eyes. But there was nothing to do.

Abruptly she sat up and stared at the TV in the corner. Unless that thing was more than just a television and had an internet connection. She might not be a computer wizard, but she was capable enough, and if she was lucky, she might discover something useful about Amber.

CHAPTER 7

Henry

Standing on the small beach not far from Leith's house, Henry stared across the calm surface of Loch Ness. He should be in the house with the others discussing what to do next to find and kill Amber, but he needed some time alone first.

The drive to Leith's house had been torture, with him trying to be pleasant and take part in the conversation amongst Trevor, Jennie, and Gawen. Henry usually enjoyed talking to people, but after what had happened with Eleanor, all he wanted was to be left alone to deal with her rejection.

Dropping his gaze to the sand covering his feet, he swallowed hard. He didn't know what he had expected Eleanor to do. She had already told him she was going to leave and couldn't help them. But for some reason, he had expected her to change her mind, perhaps because of what she had said about their chemistry the night they'd met.

He closed his eyes when he heard noises coming from the path to Leith's house. Someone was on their way to join him, but he resisted the urge to turn and bark at the person to leave him alone. His disappointment and bad mood were his own problem, and taking it out on someone else wouldn't solve anything. On the contrary, it would make him feel worse for treating the person badly.

"Alpha." Gawen's voice was soft as he stopped next to Henry. "You are in pain. Is there something I can do to help you?"

Shaking his head slowly, Henry raised his gaze to stare out over the loch again. "No. I'll join you in a little while. I just needed some time alone."

"You care about Eleanor. I take it she doesn't feel the same way about you? Perhaps she will change her mind now that you're gone. Distance can have that effect on people." Compassion suffused Gawen's voice.

"I don't think so." Henry turned his head to meet the blond man's gaze. "And it's all for the best anyway. I want to find my true mate, and although being with Eleanor would be fun, I would be running the risk of losing my focus on what I truly want."

Gawen frowned, making his blue eyes darken. "At the risk of offending you, I would like to point out that few shifters find their true mate. It's easy to forget when surrounded by all these true mated couples, but the reality is that it's rare to find the special person who's uniquely yours. Are you sure you want to give up Eleanor for a dream that might never come true?"

Henry chuckled, but it sounded hollow and sad. "If

you want the truth, then no I'm not sure. But Eleanor made it perfectly clear she doesn't want me. And I can't exactly force the woman to like me."

"That's true." Gawen's eyes crinkled at the corners when he smiled. "But I think you're giving up too easily. Perhaps there's another reason she said she didn't want you."

Henry narrowed his eyes in thought as Eleanor's words replayed in his mind. *The less you know about my sire the better. I don't want him to think he has a reason to kill you.*

There was a possibility Eleanor only said she didn't want him because she wanted to protect him. Her maker sounded like a nasty piece of work. But it was impossible to know, and Henry didn't want to pressure her when she had already told him no. She had made her choice, and he had to respect that no matter what he felt about it.

"Why don't you join us for a meal?" Gawen's question pulled Henry out of his thoughts. "It's one of the reasons I came down here to disturb you. It might help you to focus on something else for a little while."

Breathing out on a deep sigh, Henry nodded. "Perhaps you're right."

Everyone was gathered in Leith's big kitchen when they walked in. Duncan, Julianne, Michael, Steph, Callum, and Vamika had arrived from Inverness and were already seated at the table with Leith, Sabrina, Trevor, and Jennie.

There was a large pot of delicious-smelling soup in the middle of the table, and Henry suddenly realized how hungry he was. With everything that had happened in the last few days his appetite hadn't been what it usually was, and apparently it was catching up with him.

"Please have a seat." Leith indicated the unoccupied chairs by the end of the table. "I must apologize for the cramped seating arrangements, but I never foresaw having this many guests at once or more than eight children when I had this table made. A bad assumption on my part, and you can rest assured we will be investing in a longer table."

"Not with children in mind." Sabrina's eyes narrowed, and she crossed her arms over her chest as she stared at Leith. "You can trust me when I say that if you even contemplate us having eight kids or more, I will be out of here, mating bond be damned."

The whole table erupted with laughter while Leith shook his head with a slightly flustered expression on his face.

"That was not what I meant, my angel." Leith put his arm around his mate and tried to pull her closer to him. "But we are going to be together for a long time and—"

"Not long enough for eight kids." Sabrina leaned away from him with a scowl on her face, resisting his hold on her.

"I wouldn't mind eight kids." Duncan's eyes were filled with amusement as he looked at Julianne, clearly waiting for her reaction.

Julianne's auburn hair bounced around her head when she snapped her head around to stare up at Duncan. "Not unless you miraculously gain the ability to get knocked up. There is no way in hell I'm going to go pregnant eight times."

Laughter spread around the table again, and Henry

couldn't help the small smile that curled his lips. Perhaps one day he would get the opportunity to tease his mate like that. He really hoped so.

Duncan waggled his eyebrows at Julianne. "But I've heard your boobs will get—"

"Careful." Julianne's face split in a wicked grin. "Because I've heard the only surefire way to avoid pregnancy is abstinence. I think we should try it for a few days."

Duncan's amusement drained from his face. "You wouldn't be able to resist me for that long."

Lifting an eyebrow in challenge, Julianne tilted her head to the side. "With the variety of toys available these days, do you want to bet?"

Shaking his head rapidly, Duncan curled an arm around Julianne's waist and pulled her close. "No. I need you. The thought of you not wanting me is a hell of a lot scarier than facing off with Amber. Please don't even think it."

"Oh, Duncan." Julianne's eyes softened, and she put a hand on her mate's cheek. "I'll always want you. How could I not? It was a joke, big boy, and you started it, remember?"

Henry averted his eyes as the couple melted into a kiss. It was yet another thing he would love to do with his mate one day.

He had never been a fan of public affection before, preferring people to get intimate behind closed doors. But that might have had something to do with the way his parents had always flaunted their fake affection for each other when among other people. It had made him squirm with distaste and embarrassment on more than one occasion, but the main reason was probably the knowledge that it was all a charade.

"It feels like it's been weeks since we were last here, when in reality it's only been a few days." Jennie smiled as she swung her gaze around the table, before her expression tightened into a frown. "I wish we had something to celebrate, though, but with how Amber keeps evading us and becoming more dangerous every day, there's no reason for a party."

Sabrina nodded. "And unfortunately, we haven't been able to make any significant dent in her plans yet. Whatever we do to thwart her, she seems to come out stronger and more ruthless every time."

"There's plenty to celebrate, even though we haven't been able to catch the bitch yet." Trevor gave his mate a loving smile. "I found you. Nothing can ever surpass that."

Jennie's smile returned as she met her mate's gaze. "You're right. It's just overshadowed by this constant threat putting a damper on everything."

"It is." Trevor nodded. "But we'll find a way to take her down soon, and then we'll have the rest of our lives to celebrate." He winked at her.

Henry looked down at his hands resting in his lap. These couples had exactly what he wanted, and it was difficult not to feel jealous of their happiness. At least when he didn't know if he would ever have the same. Eleanor didn't want him, and what was the chance of finding his own true mate? He didn't know the probability, but he wouldn't be surprised if it was less than one in a million.

CHAPTER 8

Henry

"Speaking of Amber, we have some new information." Callum's statement made Henry lift his gaze to look at the blond wolf.

"Nothing revolutionary, I'm afraid, but still useful." Callum turned his head to look at Vamika. "Do you want to tell them about Mary? You're the one who found the information after all."

Vamika smiled at her mate before looking across the table at Sabrina. "Mary was admitted to a mental institution in Glasgow yesterday by her mother. It was around the same time as Jack's mansion blew up, which means it's unlikely Amber had anything to do with the fire."

Callum nodded before taking over. "We've managed to secure footage of Erwin's car at various times in and around Glasgow the last couple of days, which further supports our claim that Amber had nothing to do with the fire. Assuming of course that she doesn't have an accomplice and she didn't rig explosives with a timer. But none of those things seems likely based on her past behavior."

Duncan leaned forward in his seat to look at Callum. "Have you discovered what caused the massive fire?"

"No." Callum shook his head. "It's only been a couple of hours since the investigators were able to enter the ruins of the mansion. It took the whole night and well into the morning before the fire was extinguished and the structure was cold enough for the fire department to let anyone near it. We'll keep an eye on the investigation, but I doubt the findings will have any relevance for us with respect to Amber. At the moment it looks as though the fire was a separate event entirely, unless of course there's something we're missing."

"Duncan." Julianne's voice was soft, but the fear in it caused everyone to look at her and stop talking.

"What is it?" Duncan studied Julianne's face before his gaze dropped to the phone she was holding up to show him.

Henry felt his whole body tense with apprehension when Duncan's eyes widened with obvious fear and disbelief.

"I..." Duncan lifted his gaze to Julianne's for a second before turning his head to look at Trevor. "This is bad. It's a text from Amber."

Looking down at the phone again, Duncan started reading. "You will be happy to know that the limitations of the mating bond no longer exist, and you can find the evidence of that in the cottage in Queen

Elizabeth Forest Park. Prepare to be set free. Amber."

Shock reverberated through Henry's body. It was supposed to be impossible. Could Amber really have found a way to break the mating bond? If she had, it would unravel shifter society and cause complete chaos. Not to mention the personal tragedies that would ensue when mates left each other to pursue other people like humans were known to do. Betrayal and destruction of families. Henry shook his head to stop himself from getting lost in the speculations of what would happen.

"Don't panic just yet." Sabrina's eyes were narrow with anger. "She might just be trying to scare us. Or it's a ploy to lure some of us to the cottage so she can attack. That seems a bit too obvious, though. She would be stupid if she expected us to fall for something like that. And based on what she has been able to pull off so far, Amber isn't stupid."

"I hope you're right and she's just trying to terrify us. Which is working by the way." Duncan visibly swallowed. "Just the thought of losing what we have"—he shook his head slowly while staring at Julianne—"is enough to freak me the hell out." His hand came up and caressed his mate's cheek. "But no matter what happens to the mating bond, I'll still be yours. For the rest of my life."

"That's what terrifies me the most." Trevor's voice had a tremor to it that had Henry automatically bracing for impact. "Without the mating bond, there is nothing extending a human's lifespan to match their mate's."

The silence in the room was deafening. If Amber could do what she claimed, the result would be devastating for most of the couples in the room.

All eyes moved to Leith when he pushed his chair back and stood. "It is time to escalate our fight to the next level. Shifters usually deal with their own threats, but if Amber can do what she alleges, she is a threat to most of the supernatural world." Leith's gaze settled on Trevor. "I will call Aidan."

"Good call. I agree." Some of the tension left Trevor's shoulders, and he took a deep breath before he continued. "Tell him to bring the others if he can. We need all the help we can get."

Leith gave a sharp nod before he strode out of the room.

"Who's Aidan?" Jennie stared at her mate.

Trevor looked at her for several seconds before he spoke. "I'm sworn to secrecy, which means I can tell you since you're my mate, but I'm not allowed to tell everyone else in this room until I've been given express permission to do so."

Henry felt his spine stiffen at Trevor's words. There were supernaturals that didn't divulge their true nature except to a select few, and Leith was one of those. Usually it had something to do with being so unique and powerful that a lot of people would do anything to gain you as a friend or an ally, and that kind of attention would get old fast.

But this Aidan must be formidable, indeed, since two of the most powerful people in the room seemed to think he might be the answer to their problems with Amber.

Henry cleared his throat and tamped down on his mounting irritation. "So, you expect this Aidan to just swoop in and solve our problems without even needing our help?"

Trevor turned to look at him, but Henry continued before the other man could respond. "Because if he's that powerful, we should've called him earlier and prevented the death of innocent shifters."

Trevor let out a deep sigh. "If it was that simple, we *would* have called him earlier. Aidan has other responsibilities, though, that take precedence in most cases, and you would understand if I could give you the details. But the threat Amber presents has now grown to a level of significance in the supernatural world that might allow Aidan to give it priority. We'll know as soon as Leith gets back from talking to him. And hopefully, I'll then be allowed to tell you more about Aidan. As it is, you shouldn't even know his name."

CHAPTER 9

Eleanor

Eleanor was closing in on Loch Ness, and it was about fucking time. It had seemed to take forever before the sun went down so she could leave, but that was Scotland in summer. It was much easier being a vampire during winter when the nights were longer. But she didn't exactly have a choice, and she had to make do with the time she had.

Kynlee had taken Eleanor to find some clothes for her to wear, and by some miracle Hugh had left them alone while they looked for something that would fit. It was all the time Eleanor needed to use a little vampire persuasion to find out where Henry had gone. It would have been more courteous to just ask for the information, but Eleanor didn't really want Kynlee, or anyone else for that matter, to know where she was headed.

After running to the closest village, Eleanor had

borrowed a car. Technically, it was stealing, but she would make sure the owner got it back as soon as she could get herself another ride.

Driving through Fort Augustus, she headed for Leith's house by the south-eastern shore of Loch Ness. After parking in a small wooded area, she covered the rest of the distance on foot.

She had no intention of making her presence known. The only reason she was there was to keep an eye on the area to make sure Henry was safe from Amber. And if the bitch happened to show up, Eleanor would take care of her once and for all. But the only way she could do that was to go into stealth mode.

Eleanor pulled all her power into herself and locked it down tightly. Some supernaturals were extra sensitive to other people's power, and some witches had an ability to sense it, but by locking it away, she had successfully been able to hide from people like that before. And hopefully, it would work this time as well. She wasn't going to risk being caught unaware by Amber again.

After soundlessly creeping around the property to get an overview of the area, she settled down in between a few trees where she could keep an eye on the building as well as the small beach. The structure was a beautiful terraced house fitting into the sloping terrain perfectly, and without any neighbors close by.

There was light in the windows on the top level of the house, and she could see people moving around inside. It was well past midnight, but apparently these people didn't sleep much. Or perhaps they were taking turns guarding the property. Whether that would prevent Amber from attacking them undetected was doubtful, since the witch had a tendency to show up when they least expected her to.

Eleanor tried to make out who was still awake inside, but it wasn't possible to see from where she was sitting, and she didn't want to move any closer. She would have liked to know if Henry was in there or if he had gone somewhere else. But even if he wasn't one of the people moving around, it didn't mean he wasn't in the house. He could be asleep in one of the other rooms.

She pinched the bridge of her nose as her mind pulled up the last image she had of him. The pain in his eyes seemed to become starker every time she revisited the image. And she couldn't think of anything she wanted more than to find him and tell him she didn't mean what she'd said. But the reality was that she had done the right thing. Making sure he stayed away from her was the only way to keep him safe from her sire.

"You said you were in a hurry to leave, but I didn't realize this was your destination."

Eleanor whipped around so fast she knocked her shoulder against the tree next to her, causing the whole tree to sway from the impact. "Henry." Her voice was high-pitched from the shock of his sudden appearance.

Or perhaps it wasn't sudden at all. He could have been standing behind her for several minutes as far as she knew. Her focus had been on the house, and apparently she was completely shit at keeping an eye on her surroundings and concealing herself.

His jaw was tense as he stared at her with his arms crossed over his chest. There was no kindness or humor in his eyes, but then she hadn't expected there to be if she ever met him again.

"So, why exactly are you here spying on us?" His eyes narrowed, and he took a step closer. "What do you want?"

"I…" Her voice broke, and she cleared her throat before she tried again. "I wanted to be here in case Amber showed up. You weren't supposed to know."

One of his eyebrows rose, clearly portraying his skepticism. "Really? And what makes you think she wouldn't catch you this time?"

His harsh words felt like a slap, but he was right. Amber had already caught her twice, so Eleanor's track record against the witch wasn't exactly in her favor.

Then she frowned. Her power shouldn't have been easily detected after she had locked it down tightly. Taking a step closer to Henry, she crossed her arms over her chest to match his stance. "How did you know I was here?"

His shoulders stiffened, and his lips tightened into a line, making it clear he wasn't going to answer her question.

She sighed. "Okay, but can you please tell me whether you could feel my power or not from a distance? I was trying to conceal it, and it would be helpful to know whether I was successful or not."

Henry stared at her, but he didn't show any sign he was going to give her an answer.

"Fine." Eleanor turned away from him to continue her surveillance of the house and the surrounding area. "If you're not going to talk to me, you might as well leave me alone."

"Yes, I know you don't want me." His tone was

angry, but there was a note of pain in his voice that he wasn't able to conceal. If he was even trying to conceal it. "But you are the one who's stalking us and not the other way around."

She threw her hands in the air in agitation. "I'm not…"

Eleanor bit her lip when she realized what she had been about to say. Claiming not to be keeping an eye on them would be a lie. At least a partial lie. She might not have been stalking *them*, but she had been stalking *him*. "You can call it whatever you want, Henry, but I'm here to watch out for Amber. And I'm not going to stop doing that just because you discovered me. You can run back to the house now and tell all your friends I'm here. I don't mind, but it won't make me leave."

"I don't understand." The genuine confusion in Henry's voice almost made her turn around to look at him, but she resisted the urge. "Why were you so adamant you had to leave and weren't going to help us, if you were planning to follow us and watch over us? Or did you change your mind after we left?"

Squeezing her eyes shut, she contemplated what to tell him. The truth was she had been trying to persuade herself to leave him alone, but when that didn't work very well, she had settled for the second-best thing. Watching out for him without making it known that she was there. But she had failed miserably. Henry or someone else in the house had felt her presence, which meant Amber probably would too.

Eleanor turned around slowly until her gaze locked with his. "I want to kill Amber for what she did to me and other people. And…I want to protect you."

Frowning, he shook his head slowly. "If you wanted to protect us you could have just said so."

He had misunderstood her, and she should have left it at that. But for some reason she wanted him to know the truth. "Not you as in all of you, just you, Henry. I want to protect you from Amber. I just can't let her hurt you."

CHAPTER 10

Eleanor

Henry's eyes widened as he stared at her, but he didn't say anything for several seconds. Eleanor was just starting to wonder if she had misunderstood his interest in her when he moved.

He stalked toward her like she was prey, and his eyes narrowed into slits. She automatically backed away from him. But she had only taken a few steps before her back hit a tree, and she came to an abrupt stop.

It didn't stop Henry's progress, though, and he continued until he was towering over her, and his chest was less than two inches from hers. He was leaner than most of the other men in the house, but he was still a big man with plenty of muscles, and his proximity emphasized their size difference.

"Henry, please..." Eleanor's voice choked off when he closed the remaining distance between them, and she was effectively sandwiched between his hard body and the tree.

"Please what?" His eyes were practically glowing with heat when he stared down at her. "Please fuck me or please leave me alone? And be straight with me this time, because I want to know where I stand with you."

Please fuck me, Henry. Fuck me until I can no longer remember my own name. Oh, dear God, I'm going to get you killed. She swallowed hard before finding her voice again. "What I told you about my maker is still true."

She let him see the regret in her eyes. "He won't hesitate to kill you if there's any indication you mean something to me. Pure lust he can usually tolerate, but even that would be risky because he might mistake it for something more if I had sex with you more than once." *Particularly because I won't be able to hide how I feel about you.*

A small smile lifted the corners of Henry's lips. "That almost sounded like you would like to have sex with me more than once if you could. Or am I wrong?"

Eleanor chuckled to conceal how heat was spreading like wildfire through her body in response to his smile and the thick, hard ridge poking into her belly. "You might not be wrong, but that doesn't mean—"

Her voice choked off on a gasp when Henry bent his head and buried his face in the crook of her neck. He pulled in a deep breath through his nose, and desire poured through her veins like liquid fire to settle low in her belly. Wetness soaked into her panties as her channel clenched, and she squirmed.

Henry groaned as he let her go and took a step

away from her. His eyes were almost black with desire when their gazes met. "You already know I want you, but I'll respect your wish not to be intimate with me if that's your decision. But you were the one who said we have amazing chemistry, and it would be a shame not to explore that."

She tore her gaze away from his, trying to prevent him from seeing just how much it pained her to stay away from him. "I know, but I can't agree to do something that will end up hurting or killing you."

"All right, but you didn't have to lie to me."

Before she realized what was going on, she was in his arms while he strode through the trees in the direction of the beach.

"Henry, what are you doing?" She stared up at his face, but his expression was carefully blank.

"Punishing you for lying to me." He stared straight ahead. "I don't tolerate dishonesty very well."

Eleanor felt her spine stiffen with apprehension. She couldn't imagine Henry causing her any deliberate harm, but his behavior was decidedly ominous, and she had no idea what to expect.

They reached the beach, but instead of heading for the path toward the house like she had expected, he continued toward the water without slowing his progress.

"Henry?" Frowning up at him, she put her arms around his neck. If he was planning to dump her into the water, she wasn't going to make it easy for him. She might end up getting wet, but at least she wasn't going to be the only one.

"Do you like swimming?" When he waded into the water, he finally dropped his gaze to hers, and his lips stretched into a grin. But he didn't wait for her to respond before he continued. "Because I do, and I would like some company."

Her eyes widened. "I'll get wet."

Henry laughed. "That's the general idea."

She shook her head. "No, I mean my clothes. I don't have anything else to wear."

"That's a shame." Amusement lightened Henry's eyes. "But perhaps it will help you remember not to lie to me."

Before she could respond, he let go of her and dove to the side with her arms still wrapped around his neck. She let go, but it was already too late.

CHAPTER 11

Henry

Henry couldn't help laughing when Eleanor surfaced, sputtering with her wet hair covering her face. Beautiful didn't even begin to describe this woman, even when she resembled a drowned cat.

But when she rose to her feet before him, his face fell as he realized his mistake. *Good one, Henry. You're a fucking genius.*

He had expected her to get wet, but the way her white T-shirt was molded to her feminine curves, showcasing her full breasts and hardened nipples, was turning his already hard cock into granite. He had seen her naked body more than once, but this look was another level of sexy, and a temptation he wasn't prepared for. And then there was everyone else.

She had just told him she didn't have any other clothes to change into. And there was no way in hell he was going to bring her into the house looking like that. Just the thought of one of the other men seeing Eleanor's breasts on full display had jealousy spiking through him. They weren't a couple and might never be one, but she still triggered his territorial instincts.

"You know, I'm thankful that the intensity of your stare can't set things on fire, because my boobs would be nothing but ash by now."

His eyes widened in shock and shame as his gaze snapped up to hers. "I'm sorry, I… I just didn't expect…" He swallowed the bad excuse for disrespecting her before he could say it.

She chuckled. "You didn't expect my white shirt to be see-through when it got wet? Then what did you expect?"

"I… I'm ashamed to say I didn't consider all the consequences of dumping you in the water." It was embarrassing but true. And probably a result of his mind being scrambled.

Henry had been able to feel where Eleanor was from the moment she drank his blood at Hugh and Kynlee's house. And when he had felt her moving north after sunset, he had been getting more and more restless and excited the closer she got.

At first he had assumed she was going to Inverness or somewhere other than Leith's house, but when her progress paused in Fort Augustus, his heart rate sped until his pulse pounded in his ears. Was it possible she had changed her mind about him? Or was there another reason she was seeking them out?

But instead of knocking on the front door like he had expected, she had moved around the property for almost twenty minutes before settling down in one spot. Irritation and disappointment had made him decide to approach her. Because contrary to what he had hoped and expected, it had become abundantly clear that she wasn't there to see *him*.

Except based on what she had told him just a few minutes ago, she *was* there for him. Not for a romantic rendezvous, though, but to protect him. But as flattering as that was, it wasn't what he had hoped for.

"No, obviously." Shaking her head slowly, she crossed her arms under her chest, drawing his attention to her breasts yet again. "Perhaps one of the women in the house will be kind enough to lend me some clothes. Because I can't imagine them letting me walk around like this in front of their mates."

Henry growled and took a step toward her before he could stop himself. "Oh, I can guarantee there will be no parading around like that in the house." He quickly pulled off his wet T-shirt and took another step toward her to put it over her head.

"Wait." She held up her hands to stop him. "I want to get out of the water and remove this first." She fisted her hand in her wet T-shirt and pulled the fabric away from her skin.

Henry nodded while secretly missing the sight of her hard nipples poking at the translucent material. When she started wading toward the beach, he followed.

As soon as her feet met the dry sand, she pulled her white T-shirt over her head and discarded it on the beach, before reaching behind her with one hand. "Okay, you can give it to me now."

Handing over his dark shirt, he stared at her bare back. His hands were itching to touch her smooth skin, but it wasn't what she wanted. And in all truth, he shouldn't want it either. After waiting for his true mate for so long, it would be stupid to lose focus now. But his body clearly didn't care about the sensible thing to do.

Eleanor pulled his T-shirt over her head before turning to face him. "Thank you for letting me borrow another of your T-shirts, but really this time it's your own fault you're left shirtless." Her gaze lowered down his body until it settled on his groin. Her lips parted, and her eyes widened before they snapped back up to his.

He hid his smile when her eyes started glowing red. Without his shirt covering his groin the bulge of his erection was clearly visible, and the sight obviously had an effect on her. "If you want to come, I'm ready."

Her jaw dropped for a second, before she crossed her arms and scowled at him. "I already told you—"

"Inside the house, I mean." He couldn't prevent the grin that spread across his face. "Or do you want to stay out here?"

She stared at him for several seconds before she spun and started toward the house. "Let's go."

Laughing, he hurried after her. But he hadn't taken more than a few steps before he came to an abrupt stop when she suddenly turned around and blocked his progress.

Her eyes were still glowing when she closed the distance between them, but she looked more angry than turned on.

He sucked in a breath when she palmed his hard length. Even through the fabric of his jeans her touch was intoxicating.

"You're a gorgeous man, Henry, a fact I'm sure

you're well aware of. But that doesn't give you the right to taunt me when I've already told you no." Her hand stroked up his erection before giving the head of his cock a little squeeze. Then she spun away from him and continued up the path.

Fuck. His dick was throbbing, and his balls were hard and aching with his need for release. But it wasn't anything more than he deserved after what he had done to her. He was the one who always spoke of respect, but there was nothing respectful about how he had treated Eleanor since she arrived on Leith's property.

He hurried after her, until he was right next to her. "I'm sorry, Eleanor. When I felt you arrive, I thought you had changed your mind about me, but then—"

"What?!" She was suddenly directly in front of him, staring up at him with impossibly wide eyes. "What did you just say?"

Henry frowned as he repeated his words in his mind. He might have sounded a bit arrogant in his assumption that she came because she wanted him, but he hadn't expected her to react so strongly. "I didn't mean to sound overconfident or pressure you or anything, I just—"

"No." Shaking her head firmly, she narrowed her eyes at him and grabbed his wrist. "What do you mean you felt me arrive? Did you hear me?"

"No. I felt you." He cocked his head as he frowned down at her. "Can't you feel where I am? I thought that's how you knew where we had gone."

Eleanor shook her head slowly, her eyes widening with what looked like fear. "No, I can't tell where you are, Henry. And the fact that you can tell where I am…" She swallowed. "How long have you been able to do that?"

He shrugged, wondering why she looked scared. "Since the first time you bit me. Why does that scare you?"

"Could you tell where I was a few hours ago when I was still in the barn at Hugh's farm?"

Keeping his eyes on hers, he nodded slowly. "I could. Is that unusual?"

Without making any attempt to answer him, she let go of his wrist and took a couple of steps back like she needed to put distance between them.

"Eleanor, please answer me."

She nodded slowly but still didn't say anything.

Tipping his head back, Henry sighed in frustration. He wasn't sure how to interpret her reaction. Was it a bad thing that he could tell where she was at all times, or was it just unusual? One thing he was certain of, though—Eleanor hadn't intended for it to happen.

CHAPTER 12

Eleanor

Eleanor's mind was racing with fear and disbelief as she stared at the amazing man before her. She had heard that vampires could form a special bond with another person, but it was so rare it was considered an anomaly, and she had never met anyone who actually had that kind of bond with someone. Until this minute. One of the unique attributes of such a bond was that the person bonded could track their vampire's location, just like Henry apparently could with her.

The gorgeous red-haired wolf had caught her attention the first time she laid eyes on him, and he had occupied her mind most of the time since. The taste of his blood, his kindness, his amazing body. Everything about him was like it was designed to pull her in and keep her attention on him. But she had never considered it might be more than an infatuation on her part.

"Eleanor." Henry's brows were furrowed with concern. "You look scared. Can you please tell me why? Are you worried I'll follow you wherever you go from now on? I won't, I promise you."

Forcing a smile she didn't feel, she closed the distance between them before taking one of his hands in hers. "I'm not worried about that. I was just surprised, that's all. Being able to track someone is a rare side effect of a vampire bite. I've never experienced it before with anyone, and I hadn't expected it to happen to you."

He studied her face for several seconds like he was trying to decide whether to believe her or not. "It scares you, though. And don't bother denying it. It was written all over your face a minute ago."

Lowering her gaze, she nodded. He was right, but he didn't need to know why she was scared. "You need to do something for me. I want you to pretend you don't know where I am at all times. Because if someone were to find out, it would put you at risk."

Eleanor stared at his hand, strong with long fingers and visible veins on the back. But no scars since shifters didn't sustain permanent injuries. He didn't know it, but he had a chance at immortality. As someone bonded to her, he would live as long as she did if she fed from him regularly.

But she couldn't tell him that. No matter how much she wanted to keep him, it wouldn't be fair to him considering he was looking for his true mate. Robbing him of an exceptional relationship like that would be downright cruel.

He might think he wanted her, but it was most likely lust driving him as a result of her feeding from him. It was a well-known effect of a vampire bite, but it would fade with time if she stayed away from him. And hopefully his ability to track her would as well.

His other hand gripped her chin and lifted until her eyes met his. The frown on his face deepened as he studied her face. He pulled his other hand from hers, before raising it and swiping his thumb lightly under her eye. "Tell me why you're crying so I can make it right."

"I'm sorry." Eleanor took a step back, but he immediately followed, not letting her go. She hadn't even realized tears were running down her cheeks until he swiped at them. It must be in response to the knowledge that she had to let him go, but her reaction seemed out of proportion. Crying wasn't something she did, but this was the second time her tears had been running because of Henry. And the only plausible explanation was the bond between them.

He cocked his head as he stared down at her. "Why are you apologizing? Crying is neither a crime nor a sign of weakness. But there is always a reason, and I would like to know what it is so I can fix it."

If she'd had a living heart, it would have swelled in her chest. *I wish I was your mate.* She started when she realized how true that wish was.

But even if he had wanted that, she wouldn't have been able to give it to him because of her maker. And then it was the small matter of her being a vampire. She couldn't be his mate. At least she had never heard of a vampire becoming a shifter's mate before.

Forcing herself to think of how kind he was, she managed a genuine smile this time. "Don't worry about it, Henry. I don't even know why I'm crying. I guess it's just a delayed reaction to everything that's happened in the last few days."

He didn't look convinced, so she quickly grabbed his hand and turned to walk toward the house. "Come. You wanted to tell the others I'm here, didn't you? And I wouldn't mind some dry pants."

Henry didn't respond, but he gripped her hand tightly in his and walked beside her up the path.

After they entered the house at the bottom level, he led her up two sets of stairs and into a large room that was a combination of kitchen, dining room, and sitting room, with big windows and a terrace outside with a spectacular view of Loch Ness. Leith and Sabrina were there along with another couple she hadn't met before.

"I found someone who apparently wants to help us after all."

Her spine stiffened at Henry's jab, but she deserved it for spying on them. "Hi. It's nice to see you again." Eleanor nodded at Leith and Sabrina before turning her attention to the other couple, a tall blond man and a much shorter black-haired woman, who were clearly attached at the hip. "Hi. I'm Eleanor."

Sabrina smiled, and the corner of Leith's mouth tugged a little upward in something that could possibly be called a smile.

"So you couldn't resist a little witch hunting after all?" Sabrina approached with her mate right beside her. "Or was it Henry you couldn't resist?" One of Sabrina's brows lifted as she pointedly stared at Eleanor and Henry's clasped hands.

Eleanor automatically tore her hand out of Henry's grasp, but immediately regretted it. Instead of shrugging and acting like it was no big deal, she had just confirmed that it *was* in fact a big deal. *Good one, Eleanor. Perhaps you should try to act like a woman a little older than fifteen from now on.*

"I'm Callum. It's nice to meet you." The blond man approached with a warm smile and his right hand outstretched toward her. His left hand had a firm grip on his woman's hand.

"It's nice to meet you too." Eleanor smiled and shook his hand, before she turned her attention to the woman at his side.

"And this is my beautiful mate, Vamika." Callum's eyes were filled with adoration when he smiled down at the black-haired woman by his side.

Vamika beamed with happiness as she met her mate's gaze. She then tugged her hand out of Callum's grip before facing Eleanor and holding out her hand. "Nice to meet you. I hope you're here because you missed him." She nodded toward Henry, who stiffened at Eleanor's side. "Because he's clearly missed you."

Henry frowned. "Vamika, that's—"

"The truth, Henry." Vamika chuckled. "And as you have reminded me several times—honesty is essential even when it hurts or makes you feel awkward."

Eleanor couldn't help the laugh that burst from her. She should be concerned about Henry's focus on her and make sure to keep her distance from him, but she couldn't help the thrill of knowing he had missed her to such a degree that it had been obvious to the people around him. Perhaps it was all based on lust instigated by her biting him, but it still made her happy that he had been thinking about her. Because she had been thinking of him constantly.

"Fine," Henry grumbled beside her. "Do you think

one of you could lend Eleanor something to wear? She's been playing in the water." One of his brows was raised when he looked at her from the corner of his eyes.

Chuckling, she shook her head slowly. "And I wonder who's to blame for that. It wouldn't by chance be the honest one?"

Vamika, Callum, and Sabrina laughed, and Leith's lips stretched into an amused smile.

"I'll find you something to wear." The blond witch moved past them toward the door. "Just give me a couple of minutes."

"Thank you," Eleanor called after Sabrina as she disappeared out the door.

"Would you like some coffee?" Leith headed toward the professional-looking coffee machine on the kitchen counter.

"Yes, please, I would love some." Caffeine didn't do anything for her as a vampire, but she quite enjoyed the taste of coffee.

All she really needed to sustain her body was blood, but she could consume other liquids if she wanted to. Food on the other hand, was not on her menu anymore, and it was one of the things that could make her stand out among normal humans. People tended to notice if you didn't want to eat anything. But these days it was easy to blame it on a diet or an allergy, and as long as she didn't stay with the same people for long, it wasn't an issue.

"Coffee would be great, Leith." Henry sighed before adding in a whisper, like it wasn't meant for anyone else's ears. "I think I need it to get through the night."

Eleanor carefully schooled her features before glancing up at Henry's face. He looked lost in his own thoughts, but there was a sadness in his eyes that she didn't like. Was it due to her rejection, or was it because of Amber and what she was doing to shifters? No matter what was the cause, she didn't like that look in his eyes, and if there was anything she could do to replace it with happiness she would do it. Except, of course, if it involved anything romantic or sexual.

Leith had just placed a cup of coffee in her hand when Sabrina returned with a stack of folded clothes. "I wasn't sure exactly what would fit you, so I brought a selection. Hopefully, you'll find something in there that you'll like."

After taking a sip of her coffee, Eleanor put her cup on the table and accepted the clothes. "Thank you, Sabrina. I'm sure I will."

"Come." Sabrina turned to face the door. "I'll show you where you can change."

"No." Henry's voice was laced with irritation when his large hand landed on the small of Eleanor's back before pushing her gently forward. "I'll take her."

Eleanor's lips parted in surprise, but she let herself be led out of the kitchen and down the stairs before she said anything. "You're coming across as more than a little possessive, Henry. It might be time to tone it down a little."

CHAPTER 13

Henry

Henry's jaw tensed at Eleanor's words. She was right of course. But just the thought of letting her out of his sight for even a minute grated on his nerves.

He had been restless and irritable ever since leaving her at Hugh's farm, and more than once he had considered going back to her, even though she didn't want him there. If she had been another shifter, he would have taken it as a sign she was his true mate. But she was a vampire, which was a different kind of supernatural altogether, and he had never heard of a vampire being a true mate, or even a normal mate, before.

Humans and shifters mated occasionally, so he hadn't been surprised when it turned out they could also be a shifter's true mate. And since witches were inherently human by nature, the same logic was valid for them as well. But vampires weren't even alive in the sense of having a beating heart. They were moving and thinking simply as a result of magic and the energy stored in human blood that sustained them.

Henry led Eleanor into the big bathroom next to the living room and closed the door behind them before turning to her. "I'm sorry, and I know you're right, but I feel very…protective of you. You came here to protect me, remember? And I feel the same way about you."

Staring up at him with a pensive look, she chewed on her bottom lip, drawing his attention to her tempting mouth.

He had never wanted to kiss someone so badly in his life, but it was just a small part of what he wanted to do to her. The image of her naked on the bed in Hugh's barn assailed him for the thousandth time, and his breathing hitched from the sheer overload of lust that slammed into him.

Squeezing his eyes shut, he spun away from her. "Get changed." His voice was rough, and it came out more of a command than he had intended. "I'm sorry. I didn't mean it like that. Just…please change, Eleanor. I don't know what's wrong with me. I don't usually act like this. Grumpy, impatient, and possessive. It's not my style. You can ask anyone, and they'll tell you."

Sighing deeply, he let his head fall forward in defeat as the urge to hide her away somewhere she was safe warred with his need to get down on his knees and worship her. He'd never felt anything like it before.

Eleanor didn't respond, but he could hear the rustling of clothes behind him, telling him she was changing.

The seconds stretched while he waited and hoped

she would say something. A confirmation that she forgave him for his behavior would be best, but just an acknowledgement that she had heard his words would be good enough.

The noises behind him stopped, but several more seconds went by before she finally spoke. Her words weren't what he had expected, though.

"I owe you an apology, Henry. Please don't get angry with me when I tell you why."

He turned to her and took in her expression. She looked distraught and somehow guilty. But perhaps he was wrong because he couldn't imagine what she had to feel guilty about. Nothing of what had happened in the last few days was her fault.

"Okay." Tilting his head a little to the side, he nodded slowly. "I can't imagine any reason why I should get angry with you, so that shouldn't be a problem."

Eleanor winced. "Well, I guess we'll see about that. I don't know how to tell you this in a nice way, so I'm just going to be blunt. There is such a thing as a bond that can form between a vampire and someone they feed from, and I seem to have created such a bond between us. I don't know how or why or what to do about it, but I'll find out."

Henry's jaw dropped as he stared at her. What on earth was she talking about? He had heard her words, but he wasn't quite sure of the meaning. Was she trying to tell him he was tied to her? A mixture of joy and horror spun through him.

He had been told that vampires could force a bond on their victims, but he had never heard of anyone who had actually had it happen to them. Not that he knew a lot of people who had been bitten by a vampire.

"I'm so sorry, Henry." She looked devastated. "I promise I'll find a way to release you from the bond. There must be a way. We can't be the only ones this has happened to."

Taking a deep breath, he pushed his confused thoughts away and focused on what she had just told him and her body language. Her hands were fisted at her sides, and she was leaning a little back like she was expecting him to explode with rage. But she clearly didn't know a lot about what was going on, which meant this wasn't a common occurrence. "How often does this kind of thing happen? Do you know?"

She shrugged, and her body lost some of its tension. "Rarely. I don't know anyone who has had this happen to them. Up until a few minutes ago, I never even considered the possibility of it happening to me and someone I fed from."

Henry's brows furrowed. He was extremely attracted to her and didn't want to let her out of his sight for any length of time, if at all, but that didn't necessarily mean there was a bond between them. Although it would help to explain his behavior. "If it is so rare, how do you know we're bonded? Can you feel it?"

"No." She shook her head. "But the fact that you know where I am at all times is one of the unique indications of a bond. Vampires can't track each other. Not even a maker's tie to his offspring works like that."

Henry nodded. "So, that's why you looked terrified when I told you I knew where you were. I'm guessing you didn't know about the bond until then?"

Closing her eyes for a moment, she shook her head. "No, I didn't. And…I hadn't planned to tell you." She opened her eyes to stare up at him. "But it's better if you know. Unfortunately, I can't tell you much about the effects of a bond like this. But I suspect it has something to do with our attraction to each other."

Henry narrowed his eyes at her. "In which way? Is our attraction a result of the bond or is it the other way around?"

She cocked her head, and a crease developed between her brows. "What do you mean?"

He debated whether to tell her about his reaction to her scent before he even knew who she was but decided against it. There were things about his fascination with her she didn't need to know. "You caught my attention the first time I saw you coming down the stairs at Hugh's house, and you told me we had chemistry before you bit me. At least some of the attraction between us was there even before you sank your teeth into my neck and took my mind."

Eleanor's eyes widened in shock, and she took a step toward him. "Took your mind? What do you mean by that? Did I hurt you?"

Chuckling, he shook his head. "No, quite the opposite. Don't you remember what you did to me?"

Chewing on her bottom lip, she studied his face for a few seconds before answering. "I took some of your blood, and it tasted like heaven."

She narrowed her eyes in thought. "And then your friends poured into the room and pulled me away from you. I was so appalled by my own lack of control that I got out of there as fast as I could. It was cowardly, I know, but by the time I calmed enough to think straight, I was miles away."

Keeping an eye on her expression, he smiled. "I came so hard it took me a while to realize you were gone."

Her jaw slackened as she stared at him with eyes starting to glow red. "You came? But I didn't...touch you."

Grinning, Henry nodded. "Yes, you did. With your teeth. And I don't think I'll ever forget it. To be bitten doesn't have the same meaning to me now as it did before."

Her eyes were wide when she closed the distance between them and put a hand on his chest. "I wish I'd known, but I was completely lost in the amazing taste of your blood. I've never tasted anything like it before."

"So does that mean you'd like to taste me again?" He knew he shouldn't taunt her like that, but he couldn't help himself. Maker or no maker, he wanted her; it was that simple. And that complicated.

"Henry..." She sighed, closing her eyes. "I wish—"

"Henry." Callum's voice sounded through the door. "Aidan has arrived. So when you're ready, join us in the kitchen."

"We'll be right there." Henry kept his gaze on Eleanor's face, wishing they could have continued their conversation. But it would have to wait until they had talked to Aidan.

Eleanor opened her eyes and stared up at him with something resembling regret. "Who's Aidan?"

He shrugged. "I don't actually know. I've never met him before. But I think we're about to find out. He's here to help us in our fight against Amber. Are you ready to go?" He let his eyes travel down her female figure, noticing that she had changed her pants but was still wearing his T-shirt. Her feet were bare.

"Yes." Her gaze dipped to his bare chest, and she frowned. "But you need a new shirt. You can't walk around like that all night. And you need some dry pants as well."

Was there a hint of jealousy in her eyes? He thought so, but then he could be wrong. "I'll find a shirt to cover up. Don't worry." He couldn't hide the smile that tugged at the corners of his lips.

"I'm not worried." She took a step back with a guarded expression on her face and crossed her arms over her chest. "But I can't imagine the other men around here will appreciate you showing off in front of their mates."

He barked with laughter. "Showing off? Most of the men in this house are bigger and more muscular than I am, so I don't think I would be able to show off even if I tried."

Eleanor's eyes narrowed as she closed the distance between them. Her hand landed on his chest with a smack, making him wince at the sharp sting. "Don't you dare belittle yourself like that. You're by far the most gorgeous man—" Her eyes rounded a second before she spun away from him.

Warmth spread through his chest, and he wanted to strut around like he had just won a gold medal. The most beautiful woman he had ever met thought he was gorgeous. That didn't mean she would jump into his arms any time soon, but it didn't hurt his chances either.

Trying to contain his wide grin, he cleared his throat before he spoke. "Shall we go? I think they're waiting for us."

"Sure." She opened the door and hurried out of the room ahead of him, still clearly flustered with what she had admitted.

"I'm just going to change before we head upstairs, okay?" Henry moved toward his bag, which he had left by the couch in the living room. He had been trying to get some sleep there earlier, but it had been impossible with how much his mind had spun with thoughts of Eleanor.

CHAPTER 14

Eleanor

Eleanor's head was bent while she pretended not to pay attention to Henry, but her gaze never left his tall figure as he moved past her and over to the couch. He didn't turn to look at her, which gave her the opportunity to freely admire his muscular shoulders and back.

He might be right that he wasn't as big as some of his friends, but he was taller and brawnier than the average man on the street. And his looks surpassed everyone, at least in her eyes. If not for her maker, she would have been all over Henry, begging for any scrap of attention he would give her.

He pushed his pants down his legs, and she was suddenly staring at his very sexy and very naked ass. A shudder ran through her body as her need to touch him became almost unbearable. She had always loved a powerful male physique, and Henry was a prime specimen with the perfect brawny muscle to lean agility ratio.

It took every ounce of willpower she had to tear her gaze from his mouthwatering backside and lift it, only to have it crash with his as he grinned at her over his shoulder.

If vampires could blush, she would have, but the fact that she couldn't didn't help much to conceal her reaction. He had already seen her mortified expression when he caught her staring open-mouthed at his ass. For someone who was trying to keep her distance, she was doing a piss-poor job of it. But then she had never been this attracted to anyone before. And the bond probably played a part in that.

"Do you want me to turn around so you can study my front as well?" Henry winked at her.

"No!" Eleanor practically yelled the word before she spun away from him and hurried up the stairs. She needed to put distance between them. Not because she was embarrassed by his teasing but because of how much she wanted him to turn around and show her all of him. Except she wouldn't be able to keep her hands to herself if he did, and then there would be nothing to stop her from having sex with him and effectively painting a target on his chest for her sire to home in on.

She stopped at the top of the stairs and took a deep breath to calm down. It was more a mental exercise than a physical need since her heart wasn't racing with agitation, and she had no need for oxygen. But it still helped her focus on easing the tension in her muscles.

If Eleanor knew what was good for her, she would have walked out the front door and never returned.

But there was no way she could do that after finding out Henry was bonded to her. Until she figured out how to break the bond, she couldn't leave Henry's side. Not because it was impossible to do so, but because it would be painful for him. For her as well, but she might have taken her chances with the pain if she knew he didn't suffer.

A bonded needed to be fed from regularly to feel well. She had deliberately avoided giving Henry that information yet because she was dreading the effect it would have on them both. How was she going to be able to avoid fucking him when she had to drink his delicious blood every day? She had no idea. But she had to. Henry might already be doomed if her maker found out about their bond, but she was going to find a way to break their bond before her maker could find out about it.

"Thank you for waiting for me." Henry's voice reached her from the bottom of the stairs. "I thought I scared you away with my question. It was inappropriate and I'm sorry."

Pushing her chaotic feelings away, she turned to look down at him as he mounted the steps toward her. "Don't worry about it. I've done worse to you."

His gaze heated, and a small smile tugged at his lips. "You might be right, and I'll never forget it."

Instead of responding, Eleanor spun on her heel and headed toward the kitchen. The entrance was just a few feet away but by the time she reached it, Henry was right behind her.

They stepped into the room, which contained a lot more people than it had when they were there less than twenty minutes ago. Most of them were people

Eleanor had met before. Leith and Sabrina, Trevor and Jennie, Callum and Vamika, Bryson and Fia, and Gawen were all gathered at the far end of the room by the couches.

But there were another five people in the room she didn't think she had ever seen before, until one of them turned around and the shock of seeing him again made her take a step back.

Her back hit Henry's hard chest, and before she knew what was happening, his arms wrapped around her. After lifting her off her feet, he quickly transported her back the way they had come.

They were halfway down the stairs to the living room by the time Eleanor regained her ability to speak. "Henry, what are you doing?"

"If that man scares you, you never have to see him again." His voice was low and angry.

Her heart just about melted at the realization that Henry was protecting her again. But he clearly had no idea who Aidan was if he thought he would be able to stand up to the man. She didn't really know Aidan that well either, but she had seen enough of the destruction he could cause to know his powers were beyond anything she had ever encountered before or after.

"Put me down, Henry."

They had just reached the living room, and he did what she asked before spinning her around to face him. His brows were drawn tightly together in concern. "You have met him before. Did he hurt you?"

She looked down and fisted her hands at her sides as memories of the last time she met Aidan forced their way forward in her mind. "I think we should go back to the others. I'm guessing you're not the only one who wants to know why I reacted when I saw him."

Henry's hands clamped around her upper arms, causing her to look up into his angry face. "Not until you answer my question. Did he hurt you? Because if he did—"

"He didn't." She put her hand on his chest to calm him. "He doesn't hurt people unless they deserve it, so I guess he decided I didn't."

"Of course you didn't." Henry's eyes were still dark with anger. "And if he tries anything—"

Eleanor lifted up on her toes and pressed her lips to his, effectively cutting off whatever he was about to say. Kissing him was exactly what she shouldn't be doing, but she needed him to calm down, or at least distracted from his anger at Aidan. Picking a fight with someone that powerful was a bad idea, and it would only serve to draw more attention to whom she was and what happened the last time she met Aidan.

Henry groaned and wrapped his arms tightly around her, pressing their bodies together until her breasts were mashed against his hard pecs. But before he could deepen the kiss, she pulled her head back.

"We need to go back, Henry. Do you know why he's here?" She gave him the most relaxed smile she could muster.

He scrutinized her face for several seconds before he answered. "He has agreed to help us fight Amber. What did he do to make you scared of him?"

"I'm not really…scared of him. But—"

"Will you be joining us?" Leith's voice sounded from the top of the stairs.

Henry opened his mouth to answer, but Eleanor beat him to it. "Yes, we'll be there in two seconds."

Henry scowled at her. "Eleanor." There was a warning tone in his voice, but she ignored it.

"Let me go. I want to hear what Aidan has to say and how he can help us." She could easily tear out of Henry's tight hold on her if she applied a little of her vampire strength, but she wanted him to release her willingly.

He studied her face again before letting his arms fall to his sides. The scowl was still on his face when she grabbed his hand and pulled him up the stairs with her.

They arrived in the kitchen for the second time in a few minutes, but this time there were no more surprises. Everyone's eyes were on them, though, as they stepped into the room and no wonder after their hurried exit. But the one who caught her attention was Aidan.

His stare was piercing, like he was trying to read her mind through her eyes. But as far as she knew, mindreading wasn't one of his abilities. Then Aidan's gaze moved to Henry by her side, and his expression tightened into a frown, making her whole body stiffen with apprehension. Could he sense the bond between them? What would he do if he thought she had tied Henry to her against his will?

CHAPTER 15

Henry

Henry had been looking forward to meeting Aidan, but after seeing Eleanor's reaction to the man, he couldn't help the anger showing in his eyes when he met the man's gaze.

This man might be powerful, but Henry wouldn't hesitate to fight him if he found out Aidan had hurt the beautiful vampire by his side. Eleanor had claimed Aidan hadn't hurt her, but Henry wasn't convinced. Her instant reaction spoke of a bad experience involving the man.

Aidan's gaze swung back to Eleanor, and Henry couldn't take it anymore. He quickly took a step to the side and in front of Eleanor to protect her against Aidan's scrutinizing gaze. "I won't let you hurt her. I don't care who you are. I'll fight you if I have to."

"No, Henry!" Eleanor's cry sounded above the collective gasp from the people in the room, and she was suddenly in front of him, staring up at him with a fearful expression on her face. Her hands were pushing against his chest like she was trying to make sure he didn't move toward Aidan.

Then she abruptly spun around until her back was against his front. "Don't fight him, Aidan. He doesn't know who you are and what you can do. Henry's a good man. The best."

Aidan crossed his arms over his massive chest and cocked his head while he stared at them with an inscrutable expression on his face.

Every muscle in Henry's body tensed in preparation for whatever would happen next. All he knew was that he would protect Eleanor with his life if that were necessary to keep her safe.

A wide smile spread across Aidan's face. "I'm not here to kill your mate, Henry, and I don't want to fight you. But it's good to meet people who aren't afraid to stand up for the people they love. We need more of your kind."

Henry was temporarily speechless. It wasn't the response he had expected, but perhaps he should have. Both Leith and Trevor had spoken highly of the man, so Henry should have known Aidan wasn't a loose cannon or an asshole who hurt women. All Henry had to claim in his defense was that Eleanor's reaction had temporarily blinded him to that fact.

"Thank you, Aidan." Eleanor's body relaxed against Henry. "It's...nice to see you again. And thankfully under better circumstances than last time."

"That it is." Aidan nodded. "And it's nice to see you too. You look well. But then love tends to have that effect on people." A shadow seemed to flit across the man's face, but it was gone so quickly Henry wasn't sure he had really seen it.

"Oh, we don't… We're not mates." Eleanor sounded flustered when she took a step forward.

Henry immediately missed the feel of her body against his, and her words sent a jolt of pain through his body, originating from his chest. But she was right. They didn't love each other, and they weren't mates, which reminded him that he should be looking for his happily ever after instead of focusing his attention on someone who didn't want him.

At least that was what Eleanor claimed. Although, he had seen evidence to the contrary more than once just in the last hour. But no matter what she wanted, the fact remained that she wasn't his true mate, and even though he was attracted to her, a future with her would be too risky.

"Really?" Aidan's brows furrowed as he studied Eleanor's face for a few seconds before lifting his gaze to meet Henry's. The man shrugged. "If you say so."

Henry was taken aback at Aidan's apparent doubt, until he realized how Eleanor's and his behavior must have looked to everyone. They weren't mates, but their behavior could be mistaken for that kind of bond.

It might have something to do with the vampire bond they shared, but Henry didn't know what such a bond entailed. He had gotten the impression that it wasn't permanent, but it was one of the things he needed to ask Eleanor the next time they were alone. Although being alone with her seemed like a bad idea if he was going to regain his focus on finding his true mate.

"Is there anyone else that will be joining us?"

Aidan's gaze swung around the room. "Otherwise, I think we should start."

"This is everyone." Leith surveyed the people in the room. "We will not all fit on the couches by the windows, so please some of you help yourselves to chairs from the dining area so we can all sit down."

After a couple of minutes of moving couches and chairs around, they were all seated in a rough circle with Aidan the only one left standing. Henry was sitting on a chair next to Eleanor, trying to come up with an excuse to take her hand in his, even though it would be better for him to keep his distance. But no good justification came to mind, so he fisted his hands in his lap to stop himself from reaching for her.

Aidan cleared his throat. It wasn't necessary to get their attention, though. Practically everyone in the room was already staring with anticipation at the only man standing. He was tall, probably even taller than Trevor, with a muscular build and features some women would call beautiful, even though they were decidedly masculine. His blond hair was short and his eyes unusual in that one was a brilliant blue and the other was half blue and half brown.

"Before we start discussing Amber and what to do about her, I would like to tell you a little about myself." Aidan paused for a couple seconds before he continued. "What I'm about to tell you needs to stay a secret for the simple reason that our work becomes more complex the more people know about us and what we can do. And by us, I mean myself and the people I work with. We call ourselves the elemental enforcers because of how our abilities are linked to the elements."

A hand covered his, and Henry barely hid a smile as his whole body relaxed. He hadn't even realized how tense he was until Eleanor touched him. Without looking at her, he braided his fingers with hers before tightening his grip to make sure she didn't pull her hand away.

"I'm not going to describe the abilities of my fellow enforcers, since they are otherwise engaged at the moment and won't be joining us in dealing with Amber. But I'll tell you a little about my own." The tall man widened his stance and crossed his arms over his chest.

"My abilities are linked to the earth, which means I draw my power from rocks and dirt, and I can to a certain degree manipulate the earth around me. As an enforcer I act as judge, jury, and executioner of supernaturals who prey on innocent humans or other supernaturals. Witches are among the kind we pass judgment on, even though they are not technically considered supernaturals. But their powers can be as strong, and in some cases stronger than a shifter's or a vampire's, and the human police are no match for a powerful witch." Aidan's gaze traveled from one to the other of the people gathered in the room, stopping for a couple of seconds longer on Steph and Fia.

Henry noticed that Sabrina and Gawen didn't receive the same attention from the enforcer, despite the fact that both of them had powerful magic.

But Sabrina wasn't just a witch. She was a mermaid and therefore classified as supernatural. And according to Gawen's own words, he wasn't a warlock, which to Henry meant that the man had to be some kind of supernatural, even though Henry had yet to find out what kind. He assumed shifter since Gawen had mentioned he and his mother staying with a pack, but the man was more than just a wolf, if that was even part of who he was.

"How many other elemental enforcers are there?" Callum stared at Aidan with a frown tightening his features.

Aidan gave a small smile and let his arms fall to his sides. "Four including our leader." His smile widened. "And before you ask, we've been around for a while, but you won't find any records of our existence anywhere. Hopefully, we can manage to keep it that way even in this age of phone cameras and internet. In one sense, concealment is getting more difficult due to all the surveillance everywhere, but at the same time people easily dismiss authentic footage as fake or manipulated, which serves in our favor."

Trevor chuckled. "Yes. That and the fact that people don't typically believe in the supernatural anymore, claiming that everything has a natural explanation. They just don't realize that the extent of what is natural in this world is broader than they think."

"True." Aidan nodded. Then he sighed. "But let's move on to Amber. Leith has given me the short version of what you have been dealing with lately. It sounds like things have escalated quickly in the last couple of weeks. And that's one of the reasons why I agreed to help you deal with this threat to all shifters. Other reasons are the threat to humans and the possible exposure of supernaturals to the general population.

We're only five enforcers, which means we have to

prioritize the most serious threats. But I believe this is one of them. Amber might be only one person, but she's obviously both powerful and vengeful. And that's a bad combination."

"It is." Leith's brows pushed together. "And vengefulness fueled by the loss of a child is not likely to just fizzle out on its own. Even though Mary is not dead, her mind is gone, and Amber blames all shifters for what happened to her daughter."

Aidan nodded a second time. "And now she claims to have found a way to break the mating bond."

"What?" Eleanor's nails dug into Henry's hand when she tightened her grip, making him wince. "When? And how?" Her brown eyes were wide when she stared at Aidan.

"Yesterday." Julianne turned her head to look at Eleanor. "I received a text from her stating that the limitations of the mating bond no longer exist."

Eleanor's eyes narrowed when she turned to meet Julianne's gaze. "But how? She tried to use my blood to break her own mating bond, but it didn't work. And I got the impression she had tried quite a few methods before that."

"So that's why you were at her cabin?" Bryson leaned forward in his seat, his expression pensive as he studied Eleanor's face. "Did both Amber and her mate drink your blood or just one of them?"

"Both." Eleanor's tight grip on Henry's hand loosened a little, letting his blood flow back into his fingers again. "And she got really pissed off when she realized it had no effect on their bond."

A horrible thought surfaced in Henry's mind, and he felt his spine stiffen with apprehension. "Did you agree to help her break her mating bond?" Because if Eleanor did, it was a crime he wasn't sure he would be able to forgive. A mating bond was sacred and trying to break it for any reason was on par with murder in his eyes. He didn't condone arranged matings for any reason but once the mating was done, it was done, and it wasn't supposed to be tampered with.

Eleanor turned to face him before she shook her head. "No. That wasn't what I agreed to help her with."

Henry breathed a sigh of relief. But apparently it was premature.

"I agreed to try to break Mary's bond to her mate since the mating happened without Mary's consent. But I never expected my blood to have any effect. I mean why would it? If it was that simple, it would have been discovered centuries ago."

Swallowing hard, Henry pulled his hand from hers. His blood felt like it had turned to slush, slowing down as it crawled through his veins. Eleanor had committed a serious offense against his kind. She might have had what she thought was a good reason, but the effect, had it worked, would have been the complete destruction of shifter society. "I see."

CHAPTER 16

Eleanor

Eleanor froze when Henry paled and pulled his hand from hers. He didn't like what she had just told him, but she struggled to see why.

Henry was all about respect, and mating someone against their will was decidedly disrespectful. Trying to right that wrong should have been something he was all for. But for some reason, he seemed to be against it, unless there was something else that had him reacting so coldly to her all of a sudden.

Before she could ask, though, Henry abruptly rose and excused himself before storming out of the kitchen, leaving her to blink her confusion in his wake.

She turned to look at Bryson. "What did I do? I was only trying to help Mary, and as I said I didn't even think it would work."

Bryson nodded, a small compassionate smile softening his features. The man could easily be mistaken for a gang leader with his hulking frame and his prominent tattoos, but in reality he was a decent man. "I understand that, but the mating bond is as fundamental to shifters as breathing. Tampering with it in any way is on par with attacking shifter society as a whole. In other words it's unacceptable and for many unforgivable."

"Oh." Eleanor's stomach felt like it had just plummeted to the floor, and she fisted her hands in her lap as she lowered her gaze. So, she had just gravely insulted all shifters. And worst of all hurt Henry.

"I'll just…" She rose without looking at anyone and hurried out of the room.

When she reached the hallway, she stopped, not sure what to do next. Should she try to find Henry and beg his forgiveness, or would it be best if she just left?

Except she couldn't leave. The realization made her wince. Henry was bonded to her. She would need to take his blood on a daily basis until she could find a way to break the bond between them.

Eleanor sighed deeply and let her head tip forward in defeat. Telling him what the bond between them entailed was going to be awkward. But hopefully, he wouldn't object to her feeding from him until they could find a solution to their predicament, because just the thought of him hurting because of her, or any other reason for that matter, was enough to send her toward a panic.

Lifting her head, she frowned. She had to find Henry and tell him the truth about the bond. No matter his possible reaction he needed to know, and preferably with enough time to spare to let him come to terms with it before he started suffering.

Eleanor headed down the stairs. She had no way of telling where he was, but his bag was in the living room so that seemed like a good place to start her search.

She saw him as soon as she reached the bottom of the stairs. He was sitting on the couch, leaning forward with his hands fisted in his hair, and he didn't look up when she approached.

Her chest tightened as she took in his seemingly defeated position. This was her fault, even though it had never been her intention. And from what Bryson had said, she shouldn't have any hope of being forgiven.

Anger suddenly poured through her and made her lift her chin in defiance. Why shouldn't she? Why shouldn't she expect forgiveness when all she had done was try to help someone who had ended up in a terrible situation? No one deserved to be mated to someone against their will. To her it was just as bad as a death sentence, and she would have never accepted to stay mated to someone who had forced her if there was a way to get out of it.

Eleanor took a deep breath before she spoke. "I wasn't trying to destroy shifter society, Henry, but I was trying to save a young woman from a horrible fate. And I would do it again if I thought it would work."

Henry's face was marred by a deep frown when he lifted his head to meet her gaze. "But you do understand—"

"I understand that crimes like that should be punished. It's nothing better than killing someone. In fact, I think it's worse to force someone to live a life they don't want than to cause their death. If someone did that to me, I would kill that person even if it meant my own death." She spun and stormed away from him. He was undoubtedly going to object to her words, and she just couldn't stand there and listen to it at the moment without getting even angrier than she already was. And then she would probably end up saying something she didn't mean.

Eleanor raced down the stairs and out the door before heading toward the beach they had visited earlier. This was so fucked up, and she would have left if she could. It would have solved her problematic attraction to Henry, and with Aidan involved she probably wasn't needed in their fight against Amber anyway.

After quickly discarding her clothes on the beach, she ran into the water before diving beneath the surface. The cool liquid slid against her skin and slowly drained the anger from her mind.

One of the benefits of being a non-oxygen-dependent creature was the ability to dive for as long as she wanted. And she took advantage of that while swimming beneath the surface and letting her thoughts churn.

Eleanor, you're such an idiot. She had just berated the sweetest and kindest man she had ever met. Not that she didn't have a good reason to, but she could have discussed it with him in a calm and sensible way instead of letting her anger dictate her words.

She stood by what she had said, though. It was the truth the way she saw it, but she should have given him the opportunity to express his point of view. Instead, she had verbally attacked him and made it even more difficult to break it to him that she needed to feed from him before dawn.

When she finally surfaced, she was close to the western shore of Loch Ness. A car made its way along the main road heading north, but apart from that it was eerily quiet. For some reason she felt there should be more sound to accompany the danger they were facing, but the rest of the world simply didn't know what was going on. There had been a few killings that were all over the media and probably causing some people to worry, but the night was still quiet.

Eleanor shuddered as the saying *calm before the storm* popped into her mind and refused to leave. Amber was out there somewhere, planning her next move, and Eleanor wouldn't be surprised if it had something to do with the mating bond. That was what the woman had warned them about after all. The only question was whom she would target first.

A dull pain started in her abdomen and without warning her teeth lengthened and sharpened like they did when she was starving. Except she wasn't starving. It wasn't that long since she had fed from Henry, and even though it was prudent to feed every night, she could go several nights without feeding before her body started craving blood enough to cause discomfort.

"Oh fuck." Tipping her head back, she squeezed her eyes closed. It was the bond speaking, making it clear that it was time for her to feed from Henry. She hadn't expected the need for his blood to be so insistent, but it was, and it made her wonder how Henry was feeling at the moment. Did he think about her and feel a need to be close to her? He knew where she was. Would he come after her if she didn't return to him soon?

Her eyes popped open, and she stared across the water toward Leith's house. Or was Henry already in pain and wondering what was going on with him?

Eleanor dove beneath the surface again and sped toward the other side. She didn't look forward to telling him what was happening to him and why, but there was no way around it. It couldn't wait any longer.

It didn't take her long to reach the beach, and she didn't waste time on drying her body before pulling on her clothes. Using her vampire speed, she reached the door on the lower level of the house in a few seconds and yanked open the door.

Her face met a hard chest, eliciting a grunt from whoever she had hit and leaving her momentarily stunned. Blinking her eyes a few times, she tipped her head back to meet Henry's frowning gaze. "I'm sorry."

He studied her face while rubbing at his chest where she had hit him with her forehead. "Are you all right? Did I hurt you?"

Eleanor couldn't help the snort that was torn from her. "I'm fine. I think I'm the one who should be asking you those questions. My head is quite hard, and I don't get hurt easily. I heal faster than you as well. Are *you* all right?" She took in his paler-than-usual complexion and the beads of sweat on his forehead.

"Yes." With that short answer he spun away from her and headed toward the stairs.

He wasn't all right, though. That was obvious. But it had nothing to do with her headbutting him in the chest.

Pulling in a deep breath to calm the irritation at his

blatant lie about his discomfort, she followed him up the stairs to the living room. He was trying to shut her out, but if she wasn't mistaken, he had been on his way out to look for her, even though he'd known where she was. Although that might be just the bond pushing him to stay close to her.

She had expected him to continue up the next set of stairs to join the others in the kitchen, but he didn't. Instead, he moved back to the couch where he had been sitting before and sank down on it like all his energy had just left his body. His eyes closed, and his head fell back to rest against the top of the couch cushion.

Fear froze Eleanor to the spot when her gaze landed on the beads of sweat running down his face. He looked sick, and shifters didn't get sick. Could the bond really be responsible for his condition, or was this a result of something else? But if so, what? What could do something like this to a shifter?

CHAPTER 17

Eleanor

"Henry?" Eleanor quickly closed the distance between them and sank down to her knees right in front of him, putting her hands on his thighs.

He didn't react and her fear intensified. Climbing up onto the couch, she straddled his legs and clasped his head in her hands. "Henry, what's wrong?" But there was still no response. His breathing was even like in sleep, but it was more likely that he had fallen unconscious.

Swallowing hard, she stared at him. This wasn't how she had wanted to do this. She had wanted his consent this time before she bit him. But he wasn't going to be able to give her that when he was unconscious.

"Please forgive me, baby." Eleanor whispered the words before tilting his head to the side to give her access to his neck. Without hesitation, she let her teeth sink into his skin, and she groaned with pleasure when the first spurt of his blood hit her tongue.

Henry's blood was like an exquisite wine produced specifically to suit her palate. All human and shifter blood tasted good, but nowhere near as good as Henry's. His was on a different level, like the contrast between a three-star Michelin Guide restaurant and your local diner. Except food didn't usually turn vampires on like Henry's blood did to her. Her channel clenched, and she squirmed on his lap as desire heated her body.

Arms suddenly wrapped around her and tightened until her front was flush against Henry's hard chest and abs, and her clit was pressed firmly against his very solid cock. It was impossible not to move and cause some very pleasurable friction between them, and by the low growl Henry let out, he seemed to enjoy it as well.

Her relief at him being awake mixed with her need, and she ground herself against his hard length. She would have loved to be able to shower him with kisses and tell him she wanted him. Thoughts of her maker prevented her from doing that; though, she could do something else for him.

After retracting her teeth from his neck, she bit her tongue and licked Henry's wound to close it. She kissed him right beneath his ear before she whispered, "Please let me do something for you."

His body tensed, and his arms disappeared from around her. But instead of agreeing to her request, he lifted her off his lap and unceremoniously dumped her onto the couch beside him before getting to his feet.

There was pain in his eyes when he met her gaze.

"Why did you do that? You don't want me, and I don't"—his expression smoothed until it showed no emotions—"want you anymore either."

Eleanor's stomach tightened into a hard knot, threatening to expel the blood she had just drunk. The last thing she wanted was to hurt this man, but she still ended up doing so again and again.

She needed to explain what was going on, but would he believe her? It would probably sound like some lame excuse for her to prey on him without him having a choice in the matter. But then that was sort of the truth. She hadn't meant to bind him to her, but she had anyway, and now they were irrevocably tied together and dependent on each other. At least for the time being.

Henry spun on his heel and hurried away from her, but she was quicker. Before he could reach the stairs, she snagged his arm and spun him until his back was against the wall. "I need to explain. Whatever you do afterward is your choice, but you need to know the facts."

His lips tightened into a hard line, but he didn't try to pull away from her.

There was no way to break this to him in a nice way, so she gave it to him straight. "The bond requires me to drink from you regularly or you get sick. You looked sick and wouldn't wake up, so I drank, and we'll probably have to repeat that procedure every twenty-four hours or so until I can find a way to break this bond between us."

Eleanor let him go and took a step back from him. She had told him what she needed to, and now it was up to him to decide what to do with that information.

If he didn't want her to drink from him again, they would both have to suffer until she could find a cure. But so be it. She wasn't going to drink from him without his consent ever again.

Henry stared at her for several seconds without saying anything. His expression hadn't changed, making it impossible to tell what he was thinking.

Eleanor took another step back to put distance between them. She had a feeling his decision wasn't going to be in her favor, which meant she would have to focus her effort on finding a way to break the bond instead of helping in the fight against Amber. But it was already too close to dawn for her to leave. She could, however, make a few phone calls.

She broke their eye contact and dropped her gaze to the floor. "I'm sorry, Henry. I never intended for any of this to happen. And when you fell unconscious, I didn't have any other choice but to act. I should've told you what the bond required earlier, but we haven't really had much time to talk since finding out that we're tied together."

Eleanor let the seconds stretch, hoping that Henry would say something. When he didn't, she lifted her gaze back up to his.

His brows were pulled together in a frown, and he opened his mouth like he was going to say something. But before he could utter a single word, his phone rang.

Henry didn't look away from her while pulling out his phone, touching the screen, and lifting it to his ear. "Hi, Mom."

Eleanor's eyes widened, and she backed away from Henry to give him privacy while he talked to his mother. She would have liked to settle things between them immediately, but that would have to wait. And perhaps it was for the best anyway, since Henry might need some time to digest what she had just told him before they could come to an agreement. But then she already had a feeling what the outcome would be, so discussing it might not lead anywhere.

She had just put a foot on the first step to go upstairs when Henry sucked in a breath that made her stop.

"What? Can...you repeat that? I don't think I heard you correctly." The sheer horror in his voice made her turn around to look at him. He had gone pale again, but this time it had nothing to do with her and their bond.

"That's impossible. How can you be so sure it's gone? Have you talked to Dad about this?" Henry's eyes flitted from side to side, clearly not focusing on anything in front of him. All his attention was on whatever his mother was saying.

Eleanor's chest felt tight all of a sudden, like Henry's distress was somehow affecting her. Her hearing was better than a human's, and she could have listened in if she wanted to, but she usually chose not to invade people's privacy and that included Henry's.

"Mom, please don't make any rash decisions. At least wait until you're one hundred percent sure. I'll be there as soon as I can, okay?" Squeezing his eyes shut, he leaned his head back against the wall.

Swallowing hard, she stared at him and fought the urge to go and comfort him. Whatever his mother was saying was hurting him, and Eleanor couldn't help the anger she felt rising toward the woman, even though she herself had hurt him just minutes ago.

"Mom, don't go. Don't…" Henry's shoulders sagged, and he lowered his phone to stare at the screen. There was something so vulnerable in his face, and it was making her feel like she was seeing a glimpse of the boy he once was, and a side of him he didn't usually show other people.

"Is there anything I can do to help?" Eleanor took a step toward him. "I'm sorry, but I couldn't help hearing your side of the conversation."

Henry took a deep breath before letting it out in a whoosh. "I don't think there's much anyone can do." He lifted his gaze to hers, and she was taken aback when she saw the tears that had filled his eyes. They hadn't fallen yet, but that didn't really make any difference. Whatever his mother had said was bad enough that he was struggling to cope with the information.

The reservation Eleanor had felt about comforting him vanished, and she quickly closed the distance between them. Wrapping her arms around his neck, she pulled his head down to rest on her shoulder.

Her fear that he would pull away from her quickly disappeared when he wrapped his arms around her and tightened his hold until she was thankful she didn't need to breathe.

CHAPTER 18

Henry

Henry held on to Eleanor's slight frame for dear life. He felt like he was drowning, the tide tugging at his feet and trying to pull him under. The whole foundation of his existence had just been shattered, and he had no idea what to do, how to stay on his feet and keep walking. Everything he had worked for and believed in was lost, or at least it would be as soon as the news spread among shifters.

"Do you feel comfortable telling me what happened? You don't have to if you don't want to." Eleanor's voice was soft and guarded, like she was expecting him to react badly to her question.

He still had trouble accepting what she had done to help Mary, even though Eleanor had only been trying to help someone who had ended up in a terrible situation. But he doubted Eleanor had evaluated the repercussions if it had worked. Not that it mattered anymore.

"My mother is"—he struggled to force the words out—"no longer bonded to my father. Amber targeted my mother for some reason, and my parents' mating bond is gone."

Eleanor's body tensed. "I'm so sorry. How…is your mother taking it?"

Henry sighed. "She's ecstatic."

Eleanor jerked against him, clearly not expecting that answer. "Oh, I thought… I'm sorry."

"I need to go." He lifted his head from her shoulder.

Her arms disappeared from around his neck, and she took a step back. There was a frown on her face when their gazes met. "To talk to your mother?"

"Yes, I don't know if the bond can be reinstated, but—"

"Henry, are you even listening to yourself?" The red tinge in Eleanor's eyes accompanied the narrowing of her eyes in anger. "I'm sorry if this comes out harsh, but your mother was obviously unhappy being mated to your father. Why on earth would you want their bond reinstated when she's so happy it's gone?"

He flinched at her words, but they were fair questions, and from a vampire's perspective they probably made sense. "My parents are the alpha couple of the pack I grew up in. What do you think will happen when people realize they're no longer mated? And as far as we know, without any repercussions. The whole pack structure will unravel with some people wanting out of their bonds. Even though customs have changed, and most people choose their own mate these days, there are still a lot of couples who weren't given that choice. This is not about my parents but about shifters as a whole. What is ideal on a personal level isn't necessarily optimal for a whole culture."

Crossing her arms over her chest, she scowled at him. "That sounds like an excuse for forcing people to stay in relationships they don't want."

Henry ran his fingers through his hair in frustration. "I don't condone any mating that's not completely voluntary, but I have a responsibility toward the stability and continuation of shifter society. Breaking up old bonds will destabilize the whole community and create a lot of insecurity and rivalry that we don't need. There are few serious disputes between packs and clans these days, and we live relatively peaceful lives, but that will come to an end if bonds can be broken and nothing is sacred anymore."

Eleanor still didn't look convinced. "I understand that you're thinking about the greater good, but how can you dismiss all the people who are unhappy in their relationships? I get that this will shake shifter society to its core, but think of all the people who will get a second chance at happiness."

Henry stared at her. "If Amber gets her way, it's not just the unhappy relationships that will be broken. All bonds will be ripped away, and I for one shudder to think what that will do to people, particularly the happy ones. It will yank the foundation out from under their feet. Mistrust and jealousy will become the norm even among previously happy couples, and I can't stand by and let that happen, no matter if it means that the people currently unhappy with their mate will have to stay bonded. It's a price I'm willing to pay."

"What about our bond?" Her expression had gone blank as she stared at him.

He frowned. "What do you mean?"

"We're tied together until I can find a way to break the bond. It's not the same as a shifter mating bond. Although I don't know enough about it to be sure how it would develop over time if we embraced it. But what if you were mated to me for life? It happened against your will, and you wouldn't be able to change it. How would you feel about me for taking your opportunity to find your true mate away from you?"

Henry froze. He hadn't considered the vampire bond an obstacle at all with regard to finding his true mate, but from her words she didn't sound sure about what the bond meant. And what if she couldn't find a way to break it? "Do you think there's a possibility we'll be tied together forever? I was under the impression that breaking our bond was only a matter of finding the correct procedure to do so."

Eleanor bit her bottom lip, and her gaze slid away from his, like she suddenly regretted having brought up their bond at all. "I don't know." Her voice was low. "I wish I could tell you that it's only a formality, but I can't. I simply don't know, but if I can borrow your phone, I'll make a few calls. It shouldn't take me too long to find out… I hope."

That didn't sound very reassuring, but there wasn't much he could do about it. "Here." Henry held out his phone. "Make the calls necessary to find out." He met her gaze with a neutral expression when she accepted the phone from him. His future was in her hands, and he didn't know how to feel about that.

Or he did, but he wasn't sure if it was just the

vampire bond affecting him. His heart was beating double time in his chest, and he was working to prevent his lips from stretching into a wide smile. He should be concerned, but the thought of a bond tying them to each other for life was oddly thrilling.

It wasn't what he should be feeling, though. His focus should be on finding his true mate. Or rather destroying Amber, and *then* finding his true mate. That way his future would be secured.

Eleanor turned away from him before disappearing down the stairs to the bottom level of the house. He walked to the windows when he heard a door close downstairs. She soon became visible as she strolled toward the beach with his phone to her ear.

Henry let his eyes linger on her feminine form. The attraction he felt toward her was more profound than he had ever felt for anyone. She was beautiful and enticing, but that wasn't all. Her consideration for other people and her willingness to help somehow enhanced her beauty in his eyes.

He might want to preserve the shifter mating bond as it was, but he still agreed with some of her arguments against it. A mating bond became destructive when forced upon someone, and no one should have to experience that. But a bond created with love was something to be cherished and celebrated.

A sudden thought made him shudder, and he regretted offering her his phone. What if she actually found a way to break their bond? What would happen then? Would his attraction to her die with the bond, or would he be left yearning for her when she merrily went on her way to continue her life without him?

"Fuck!" Henry scrubbed his hands down his face. He couldn't remember ever having felt this torn. His purpose and goal had always been so clear, but now he didn't know which he wanted more—his true mate or Eleanor? Because he couldn't have both. And realistically he might not be able to have either. The probability of finding his true mate was low, and Eleanor had been adamant she didn't want him, even though she acted like she did.

"Is she your mate?" Bryson's voice startled him and made him aware of the man's footsteps coming up behind him.

"No." Henry shook his head.

"Do you want her to be?" The big panther alpha stopped beside him, and Henry turned his head to meet Bryson's gaze. A small smile lifted the corners of the man's lips.

"I…don't know." Sighing deeply, Henry turned back to keep an eye on Eleanor through the window. She had reached the beach, his phone still plastered to her ear. She was still on the same call, and he couldn't help thinking that it was a bad sign. If the person she was talking to didn't know how to break the bond, Eleanor would have said goodbye and moved on to the next person on her list.

"Are you sure about that?" Bryson chuckled. "Because the way you keep looking at each other and touching each other, you could have fooled me."

Henry didn't know what to say. Bryson was right. With the way he and Eleanor had been acting, it was no wonder people got the wrong idea about them.

The other man's voice was serious when he continued. "You shouldn't hold it against her that she tried to help Mary. Most people who aren't shifters would have done the same."

Frowning, Henry turned to look at Bryson again. "No. Most people wouldn't have followed a woman they didn't know to save someone they had never met. But Eleanor did, because she cares more than most people."

Bryson laughed. "Okay, so you're not really holding that against her then. Good to know. Then what's stopping you from pursuing her? Is it the fact that she's a vampire?"

"Of course not." Henry scowled at the other man. "I don't care about that. But..." He stopped himself, not sure how much to tell Bryson about his hopes and doubts, and generally mixed feelings. But perhaps that was exactly what he needed—someone else's perspective.

"I should be looking for my true mate." Henry swallowed thickly. "And Eleanor says she doesn't want me."

CHAPTER 19

Henry

The boom of Bryson's laughter filled the room and made Henry cringe. Perhaps telling the previous womanizer who'd had thousands of women drooling over him hadn't been such a great idea.

"Trust me when I tell you, Henry, that she wants you. I don't care what she says, because her actions speak volumes. You might as well be God in her eyes. If she says she doesn't want you, there's an external factor making her push you away."

Henry studied the other man's face. There were those who considered Bryson a big brute with no brains, but that was far from the truth. "She says her maker will kill me if he thinks I mean anything to her, and apparently her maker is a nasty piece of work."

"Well, there you go." Bryson grinned. "You have your answer. We'll help you take care of her asshole maker, and she will be free to do as she wants without fearing for your life."

Henry sighed. "There's a complicating factor. The first time she bit me, she ended up tying me to her, and I don't know if some of our attraction to each other is due to that bond."

Frowning, Bryson crossed his arms over his chest. "She tied you to her without your consent? That's—"

"It wasn't her intention."

"Really? Are you sure about that?" Bryson had one eyebrow raised when he studied Henry's face.

Crossing his arms over his chest and widening his stance, Henry gave a sharp nod. "I'm sure. She didn't even realize we had a bond until I told her I've had the ability to pinpoint her location since she first drank from me."

The panther alpha's jaw dropped, and he stared at Henry with wide eyes for several seconds before he seemed to pull himself together. "You can tell where she is? Can she do the same to you?" Then he frowned. "I guess not since she didn't know about the bond."

"Exactly. Eleanor didn't know, and she became scared when I told her, and she realized what had happened. You can't fake that kind of reaction."

Henry turned to look out the window again. Eleanor was still standing on the beach. "But it makes things complicated. I was attracted to her before she bit me the first time, but since then...I don't know what I'd be feeling without the bond. But then it probably won't matter for much longer. She's out there talking to someone to try to find out how to break the bond between us. So, I guess I'll have my answer soon."

"You don't sound happy about that." Henry could hear the frown in Bryson's voice.

Henry sighed again. "I should be, because then I might be able to forget about her and return my focus to finding my true mate."

Bryson didn't reply, but he didn't leave either, and for that Henry was thankful. This whole situation was getting to him, making him tense and jittery, but he felt a little better after having told the other man what was going on. And he knew he could rely on Bryson no matter what happened next.

The conversation with his mother popped into Henry's mind, and he turned to look at the panther alpha. "Amber has already started destroying mating bonds."

Bryson's head snapped around, and his eyes narrowed when he met Henry's gaze. "How do you know?"

Henry put his hands in his pockets before looking back at Eleanor. "My mother called. She's no longer mated to my father."

"Fuck! I'm sorry." Bryson's hand gripped Henry's shoulder in a comforting squeeze. "Go to her. We can handle things here." Then he paused for a few seconds before he continued. "No, we should all go. Now that we know Amber's latest location, we can track her from there. Because I'm assuming this is a recent occurrence, and your mother wasn't far from pack lands when it happened."

Henry nodded and turned to look at Bryson. "That's right. My mother is still up north. She's packing her things as we speak and will be heading to Inverness as soon as she's ready."

"Then you should meet her there." Bryson's gaze was filled with compassion. "We'll take care of Amber. Don't worry about that. It sounds like you have enough on your plate already without worrying about a crazy witch."

Henry snorted. "Yes, it would seem that way." Then he sobered. "I'll talk to Eleanor. Unless we can break the bond between us easily, she'll have to come with me. Apparently she'll have to drink from me regularly while we're bonded or I'll get sick."

The panther's eyes widened with surprise. "It sounds like a vampire bond isn't nearly as much fun as a shifter bond. Damn. Talk about getting the wrong end of the stick."

Laughter burst from Henry. Bryson had a way of putting things into perspective sometimes. The man obviously hadn't been bitten by a vampire before. Henry frowned. Except he had. Eleanor had drunk from Bryson right after they found her at Amber's cabin.

Jealousy slammed into Henry at the mental image of Bryson enjoying Eleanor's teeth embedded in his skin. He growled, and his hands were around the other man's throat before he could stop himself.

"Whoa," Bryson croaked, his hands closing around Henry's wrists.

Henry's heart was slamming against his ribs when he forced himself to loosen his grip and remove his hands from around Bryson's throat. "I'm sorry. I…" He backed away a couple of steps. "Fuck." *I'm turning into a lunatic.*

Henry swallowed down the remnants of his jealousy and anger. From Bryson's comparison between a vampire bond and a shifter bond it was evident that the panther hadn't had the same experience with Eleanor's bite as Henry had. And Bryson only had eyes for one woman, his mate, Fia. But Henry's jealousy had made him forget all that and attack one of the people he respected the most.

"It's okay." Bryson rubbed his throat.

"No, it's not." Henry sighed. "Attacking people without a good reason is never okay. Please forgive me. I don't know what's wrong with me at the moment."

Chuckling, Bryson rolled his eyes. "Between the brunette out there and your mother, you have more than enough reasons to claim temporary insanity. Run with that and I'll forgive you."

"Thank you, I think I will." Henry smiled and swung his gaze back to the beach, only to realize that Eleanor had just started up the path toward the house. She was coming back, and she was no longer speaking on the phone. He might as well be waiting outside the door to purgatory for the fear that threatened to paralyze him.

"I'll go upstairs and tell the others that we have proof Amber can destroy mating bonds." Bryson's hand landed on Henry's shoulder again. "But I won't tell them who just had their mating bond broken. I'll tell them it's a trusted acquaintance of yours."

Henry nodded and glanced at Bryson. It was important that the others were told about the development, but he had a feeling Bryson also used it as an excuse to leave Henry and Eleanor alone to talk.

A door on the bottom level of the house closed just as Bryson started up the stairs. Apprehension filled

Henry's veins with shards of ice that cut and stabbed him as they were pumped through his heart. *Please don't tell me you know how to break our bond.*

CHAPTER 20

Eleanor

Eleanor stopped right inside the door and closed her eyes to try to get a handle on her emotions. It was like she had been jolted by high-voltage electricity, making all the nerve endings in her entire body jump and spasm with nervous energy.

She had been taking her time while walking the short distance from the beach to the house to think about what to say, but she hadn't come up with a good way to convey her message to Henry, and she was dreading his reaction.

"Are you coming up or are you going to stay down there?"

Henry's voice from the top of the stairs startled her and stopped her mind from spinning out of control with anxiety.

"You can do this," she whispered as she took her first step toward the stairs.

He was standing at the top of the stairs, waiting for her, and she met his gaze while making her way up one step at a time. His expression was carefully schooled, but there was no hiding the tension in his jaw.

Eleanor didn't want to do this. She didn't want to see anger and disappointment in his eyes, but as with so many things, she didn't have a choice. He needed to know what she had found out so he could deal with the consequences.

Henry waited until she was close enough to touch him before he moved back and let her take that last step up onto the living room floor.

Without saying anything, she moved over to the couch and sat down. She needed to sit down for this, if for nothing else than to hide her knees shaking.

Henry sat down next to her and studied her face without saying anything. He was obviously wondering what she had found out, but he didn't push her.

There was no easy way of telling him, so she might as well blurt it out and deal with the consequences afterward. "I can't find anyone who knows how to break the bond, Henry, or if it even can be broken. I'm sorry."

His lips twitched before he abruptly turned his head away from her so she couldn't see his face.

Had that been what it looked like? She could have sworn he had just stopped himself from smiling. But that made no sense. He should be disappointed or angry or...something. But not happy.

"Henry, did you hear me?" She put a hand on his forearm. "I said—"

"I heard you." He turned back to her with a wide grin, making her jaw drop in astonishment. "And I know it's not what you wanted, but I can't help feeling privileged that I'll be able to spend more time with you. We are bonded at least until further notice, and I'd like to spend that time to get to know you better."

Eleanor closed her mouth with an audible clack. He had said he wanted her, but she had assumed he wanted his freedom more and a chance to find his true mate. Perhaps he was still expecting this to only last a few days until they found a way to break the bond. "I'll keep searching for a way to break the bond, but I hope you realize there might not be one. We might be stuck together forever."

Henry was still grinning when he nodded. "I understand that, but let's take one day at a time, shall we? I don't mind being stuck with you for the time being, and whatever happens down the line, we'll deal with it then. But until then"—his gaze traveled from her face slowly down her body—"we should spend our time together wisely."

Every part of her ignited with the heat shining in his eyes. The attraction she had tried to keep at bay exploded through her system, making her nipples tingle as they tightened into hard peaks poking at the fabric of her shirt. She wasn't wearing a bra since the one Sabrina had given her didn't fit.

Henry growled low in his throat when his gaze landed on her chest, and she shuddered as the sound seemed to caress her most sensitive parts.

He lifted his hand slowly, and she bit her bottom lip while following it with her gaze as it moved toward her left breast. But his hand stopped when an inch separated it from her aching nipple, and she lifted her gaze to his.

One of his eyebrows was raised in question, and she nodded quickly to give him permission to touch her. The rising tension between them had left her temporarily speechless, so she sincerely hoped he didn't require her to voice her consent.

Henry cupped her breast, and she sucked in a breath as his strong, warm hand kneaded her flesh, and his palm pressed against her nipple.

A spark of pleasure shot directly to her clit, and she squirmed as need flooded her and pushed all her reasons why they shouldn't do this to the back of her mind. All that remained was her insane attraction to this amazing man.

His hand on her breast disappeared, and he grabbed her hand as he stood. "Come. Let's go somewhere a little more private."

She rose and let him guide her to the bathroom they had been in before. Once they were inside, he locked the door behind them before he stalked toward her with a wicked grin on his face. The sight of him like this with the predator part of him shining in his eyes was stunning. And so dangerous to her sanity.

"Henry." She breathed his name, her eyes locked with his as she backed away from him. Not because she didn't want to be near him, but due to what being near him would do to her. All she wanted was to be locked in his embrace and lose herself in his kisses, but she knew without a doubt that giving in to him would change her forever. No matter what happened to the bond between them, she would never be able to forget him.

Her back hit the wall, and his grin widened as he closed the distance between them. He placed his hands on the wall on either side of her shoulders before pressing his taller body against hers, making her feel vulnerable and safe at the same time. A strange combination but it was what he did to her.

Her gaze dropped to his mouth when he bent his head toward her. But just before their lips met, he moved his head to the side and nipped at her jaw. She jerked at the thrilling sensation of his teeth against her skin, and her channel clenched in a silent request to be filled.

"Henry. If you want me to catch fire, you're doing a really good job. At any other time, I'd love for you to take your time with me and tease me, but not this first time. I want your cock inside me. Now."

Chuckling, he pulled his head back to look at her. "So impatient. What if I need some time to warm up?"

"You don't." She pushed her hand between them and palmed his hard length through the fabric of his pants. "You're so hard, you could kill a man with this thing. Or a woman."

"Well, I can think of more pleasurable ways to use that thing." His eyes glittered with amusement as his hand curved around the back of her neck.

His lips descended on hers, and she arched into him when his tongue pushed into her mouth. He tasted so delicious, and he had a way of dominating her mouth that spoke to her need to be taken care of.

Henry was a kind and caring man, but he was also an alpha obviously used to taking charge. Some might think him a pushover because of his calm and caring behavior, but that would be a mistake.

He broke the kiss a millisecond before spinning her around and pushing her front against the wall. After gripping her hands and locking them against the wall above her head with his own hands, he leaned in and bit her earlobe lightly.

Eleanor jerked as pleasure raced through her. She loved teeth against her skin. A lot of vampires had a thing for teeth and being bitten, and she was no exception.

Henry's hard body molded to her back, his shaft pressing against her ass. "I've wanted you from the first time I caught your scent. Your unique fragrance turned my cock to steel in an instant, even though I didn't even know who I wanted to fuck yet. It was disconcerting, to say the least. But now here you are at my mercy, ready to take my cock. Yet I'm going to make you wait a little longer while I explore your pussy. I want to get a feel for what you like and how you respond before I plug that hole between your legs with my shaft."

CHAPTER 21

Eleanor

Her eyes went wide, and her knees started shaking, with how much his words turned her on. It was a good thing she didn't need to breathe, because she wouldn't have been able to even if she tried.

Henry let go of her hands, but she kept them where they were on the wall. She had a feeling she would need the support to stay upright with whatever he had planned.

Kneeling behind her, he slowly tugged her leggings and panties down her legs. "Lift your foot." His hand caressed her ankle, and she lifted her foot to let him remove her clothes. "And the other."

She did as she was told and was soon left bare before him. Not entirely bare since she was still wearing a shirt, but for some reason she felt more naked than she ever had.

Or perhaps vulnerable was the correct term. Henry

had already seen her naked several times, but this time felt different. He meant more to her now than he had before, and just the thought that he might not like what he saw was enough to send a shiver of fear through her.

"I've got you, beautiful. You can count on that." His warm hands gripped her ankles for a second before traveling slowly up the back of her legs, caressing her skin on his way toward her center.

She shivered again, but this time it had nothing to do with fear. His hands soon had her panting with how much she wanted them to reach their destination between her legs.

Rising behind her, he cupped her ass. "Widen your legs, Eleanor." His hot breath fanned over her ear when he spoke. "I need full access."

Nodding, she moved her feet apart. And no sooner had she moved than Henry's hand dove between her legs from behind. His fingers slid through her wet folds before circling her swollen clit. Need heated her blood and made everything inside her tighten, and the guttural sound she let out was like something an animal would make and not a woman.

His other hand trailed up her side beneath her shirt before cupping her breast. Then he pinched her nipple at the same time as he pushed two fingers inside her, and she automatically clamped her thighs together as a spike of pleasure shot through her.

"Oh fuck," he rasped next to her ear, before his teeth nipped at the sensitive skin at the crook of her neck. "I might've made a mistake."

Eleanor froze. What did he mean by that? Had she done something he didn't like? Something that caused him not to want her anymore? She wanted to ask, but she didn't want to know the answer. But before she could decide what to do, he continued.

"It should be my dick inside you and not my fingers. I'm jealous of my own fingers right now since they get to have all the fun. But you have to open your legs again, beautiful, to allow me more room to maneuver."

A smile spread across her face, and she breathed a silent sigh of relief as she widened her legs. She would have to think of a way to punish him later for scaring her like that.

All thoughts seemed to leave her mind when he started pumping his fingers leisurely up inside her, massaging her walls as he moved. His finger joints grazed the sensitive area of her front wall, and she fought the urge to slam her thighs closed again when pressure started building inside her.

"I think you like that." Pressing his hard cock against her hip, he nipped lightly at her skin again.

Mewling with how frustratingly close she was, she rocked her hips. "Please, baby. Faster."

He was teasing her and drawing this out, and he knew it.

Henry chuckled against her ear. "Do you want to come?"

"Yes." She gasped the word as she rocked her hips faster, trying to encourage him to give her the release she so desperately needed.

His other hand let go of her breast and traveled down her body until it slid through her curls and over her clit.

"Oh, yes. God, yes." Everything inside her

tightened.

"Not God. Henry." His fingers moved faster until she was right on the edge. Then he bit her neck lightly and sent her spiraling into heaven.

Pleasure pulsed through her body for longer than she had ever experienced before, robbing her of the ability to stand. If not for Henry holding her securely, she would have landed in a heap on the floor.

"Henry?" Bryson's voice sounded through the door. "Are you in there? We're getting ready to leave. Callum and Vamika have found out where Amber is staying up north."

"Fuck." The word was barely a whisper against her ear, but it conveyed all of Henry's frustration. "We're here. I'll be out in a minute."

"Two minutes." She met Henry's gaze over her shoulder.

Bryson's laughter sounded through the door. "Just be quick, okay? I'll try to fend off any questions."

"Thank you, Bryson." Eleanor took in the desire burning in Henry's eyes. They might need to leave, but not before she had given him something to tide him over until they could find more time to be alone together.

CHAPTER 22

Henry

"We should go. The others are waiting for us." Henry removed his fingers from Eleanor's tight pussy and took a step back. What he wouldn't give to rip his pants open and push into her wet welcoming body. To pump into her until she came screaming on his cock.

Absently, he lifted his hand and put the fingers he had just used to make her climax into his mouth. His eyes closed when her taste exploded on his tongue, and he groaned as another wave of raw need slammed into him and made him stagger. The next time they had more than a minute to themselves, he was going to eat her pussy until she begged him to stop.

His eyes flew open when fingers snapped open the button of his jeans and pulled down the zipper. Eleanor's eyes widened when his dick sprang free, and he smiled at the way she stared at his throbbing member.

Then she licked her lips, and his breathing choked off as he almost came right there. He should tell her to wait until they had more time and he could worship her properly. But he couldn't get the words out. Not when she was staring at his cock like it was a delicious gourmet meal after she had been starving for a month.

She reached out and caught a drop of precum with her finger before she put it into her mouth and moaned.

"Are you trying to make me spill without touching me? Because you might actually succeed." His voice was rough with need as he stared at her mouth.

Her lips stretched into a wide smile. "That would be an interesting experiment, I'm sure. But I think we'll leave that for another time."

Before he could respond, she bent and licked his shaft from base to tip, and he had to lock his knees to prevent his legs from buckling as heat burned through him. Her soft hand cupped his balls, massaging gently and making him wonder if it were possible to catch fire from raw lust.

Then her lips wrapped around the tip of his cock, and he was lost to the sensation. Pleasure more intense than he had ever felt crashed through him, burning his veins with liquid fire as he pumped his seed into her mouth. A roar almost shattered his eardrums, but he couldn't care less if the whole house knew what was going on. This was all that mattered. Eleanor and what they were doing together.

His breathing was still erratic when he finally managed to focus enough to open his eyes. His back was against the wall with Eleanor's arms wrapped around him holding him up. He'd moved, or had been moved; he couldn't remember. But it made no difference.

She lifted her head from where it was resting against his chest and grinned up at him. "I think you liked that."

Nodding slowly, Henry gave her a small smile. "I did. Very much. Thank you." He lifted his hand and brushed a stray lock of hair away from her face. "You look beautiful with my cock in your mouth." Her eyes widening made him laugh. "And at all other times."

"Well, the cat's out of the bag." Bryson's voice was dripping with amusement. "Explaining away your roar was an impossible feat even for me. I'm sure the house shifted on its foundations. But I think you'll have to leave whatever else you had planned for later. We need to go."

Henry laughed. "We'll be right there. One minute, and this time I mean it." Should he be embarrassed that he'd just alerted the whole house to what they were doing? Perhaps. But he wasn't going to be. They had all seen his attraction to Eleanor, and even if she wasn't his true mate, she meant something to him.

Bryson chuckled. "Make sure you do."

They cleaned up quickly before heading upstairs to the kitchen. The only people there were Bryson and Fia.

"The others have already left. Except Leith and Sabrina who are outside." Bryson rose from the couch with a grin. "I guess they didn't want to stick around for a possible round two."

Henry scowled at the big man. "Shut up. I seem to remember someone's roar scaring all the cattle on Hugh's farm."

Fia gasped. "You heard us? Why didn't you say anything?"

Lifting one eyebrow, Henry gave Bryson a flat look. "Because unlike someone I know, we didn't want to embarrass you."

Fia's eyes narrowed at her mate. "I guess sex is off the menu for a few days until you learn to behave."

"Don't even think it." Bryson's arm wrapped around his mate before yanking her close and kissing her hard.

The red-haired witch struggled for about half a second before throwing her arms around her mate's neck and kissing him back.

Henry turned his head and smiled down at Eleanor by his side. "Let's go outside and see if we can find Leith and Sabrina. I assume they're out front getting ready to leave."

Eleanor nodded, and they headed outside to find Leith and Sabrina in the large garage, lining the back of Leith's large SUV with black plastic and thick blankets.

A smile spread across Henry's face when he realized what they were doing. "Thank you." He hadn't even considered the fact that the sun would rise in less than an hour when Bryson told him they had to leave. But then he had been otherwise pleasantly occupied at the time.

Leith turned to look at him. "You are welcome." His gaze swung to Eleanor. "It needs your approval, though. Do you think this will suffice to protect you from the sun?"

Eleanor's face brightened in a smile. "I do. As long as I'm not subjected to any direct sunlight, I'll be fine, and it looks like you've done an excellent job of covering all the windows in the back as well as the access from the front."

"Then I think it's time we left." Sabrina rounded the back of the car toward them. "Our luggage is already in the back. So, if you're ready…" A small smile curved her lips.

"We are." Henry nodded.

After putting his bag in the back, he climbed into the back seat, and Eleanor got in next to him. They wouldn't be able to watch where they were going, but the blankets separating the front seats from the back would allow them to have a conversation with Leith and Sabrina.

A thrill raced through his body when he realized what a lack of visual contact with the people in the front seat meant. Getting crazy when other people could listen in wasn't an option, but the privacy would allow them a few liberties.

And he'd rather focus on Eleanor and her sinfully perfect lips than think about the inevitable meet-up with his mother. He needed to talk to his mother and find out how Amber had destroyed his parents' mating bond, even though it was the last thing he wanted to do at the moment.

Henry hadn't been back to see his parents at all since he left to take over his own pack. His excuse that his new pack demanded all his attention had been valid, but he could have made time to visit his parents if he had wanted to.

A hand smoothed up his chest, and he turned his head to meet Eleanor's warm smile. All he wanted was to continue where they had left off in the bathroom, but he was better off not thinking about that until they had the opportunity to be completely alone. Walking around with an erection was a bit of a nuisance, not to mention distracting, and he had to make sure his focus was one hundred percent on what was happening when they met Amber again, and not stuck in a fantasy of fucking the beautiful vampire next to him.

Eleanor's hand curved around the back of his neck before she pulled him toward her, and he was more than happy to oblige. Soft lips met his, and he sighed with contentment at being so close to her. Her resistance to him was gone, and he might have the vampire bond to thank for that. They had to stay together as a result of the bond and what it required, which meant that Eleanor's earlier plan to stay away from him to protect him from her maker was no longer possible.

Henry nibbled on her bottom lip, and she shuddered in his arms. He had discovered that she liked to be bitten, and he enjoyed using his teeth on her, but he was going to have to be careful during sex to not accidentally mate her.

For some reason the idea of Eleanor as his mate didn't feel wrong. But he knew it wasn't an idea he should be entertaining. They were from different worlds, and although they were attracted to each other, planning a future together was a lot more serious than having a little fun for a while. And that was all without considering his goal of finding his true mate.

"The fact that we cannot see you is not an excuse to get naked." Leith's voice was stern, but there was a hint of amusement in his tone.

Henry laughed as he pulled away from Eleanor and met her gaze. "Don't worry, Leith. We won't have sex in the back of your car."

"Good. Please do not mistake my comment for disapproval. It is not. It is time you acted on the attraction between you two, and I am happy for you."

Henry froze, and from the way Eleanor's eyes widened, she seemed stunned as well. He felt like Leith's comment required a response, but Henry didn't know what to say. *Thank you* would have been natural if he had intended to mate Eleanor. But since he didn't, Henry needed to come up with some kind of noncommittal response.

"Thank you for saying that, Leith." Eleanor smiled at Henry. "I wasn't sure any of you would approve of me after everything that's happened. I want to do what I can to help you kill Amber. Hopefully, with Aidan's help we'll be able to complete that task before she can do any more damage."

Henry relaxed and returned Eleanor's smile. She had managed to be gracious while steering the conversation to another topic. He quickly squashed the little sting of hurt that she didn't openly proclaim she was happy to be with him.

"Yes, I agree." Sabrina's soft voice flowed through the blanket. "And I'm really sorry to hear about your acquaintance, Henry. Have they tried to reestablish the bond?"

CHAPTER 23

Henry

Closing his eyes, Henry pulled in a deep breath. Bryson had wanted to protect him by not telling everyone who it was that had had their bond broken. But it would only be a matter of time before they found out the truth anyway, so he might as well come clean now and save himself the awkwardness later.

"No, they haven't." Henry opened his eyes and stared at the blanket in front of him. "And I'd be very surprised if they did. My parents have never been a happily mated couple, and my mother is ecstatic that the bond is gone, and she doesn't have to spend time with my dad ever again if she doesn't want to. And she will never want to."

No one said anything for several seconds. The only sound that could be heard was the rumbling of the car engine.

"I am so sorry to hear that." There was concern in

Leith's voice. "I do not know them well, but I had the impression they loved each other."

Henry chuckled, but there was no amusement in the sound. "Yes, that's what they wanted everyone to believe. It's one of the few things they actually agreed on. Appearances were everything, but the reality was vastly different. If they could have pretended to us kids as well, they probably would've. But living a lie twenty-four hours a day was too much even for them."

Memories of his childhood assailed him. The lie they had all had to live to protect their parents' reputation. He had always hated it, making it impossible to respect his parents and their leadership. Which in turn had made it easy to leave the pack and take on new responsibilities when the opportunity presented itself.

Henry hadn't even been ten years old when he had promised himself he would never end up in a situation like his parents. He would rather die than mate someone he didn't love and who didn't love him back. And the only way to secure that was to find his true mate. Yet here he was, giving in to his body's desire for a beautiful woman who wasn't his future.

"It sounds like a less-than-happy upbringing." Leith's voice was soft. "I take it they were not given a choice in the matter of who to mate."

"My father was, and he chose my mother. She was delivered to him, even though she loved someone else and didn't want to mate my father." Henry could hear the resentment in his own voice. "To say they had a bad start is an understatement, and they didn't grow to love each other over time either. I need to talk to her, though, to see if there is anything that can be done. I still can't get behind the destruction of mating bonds. No one should be mated against their will. But giving people an option to leave each other once mated will go against all our customs and destroy our whole culture."

Eleanor's arm disappeared from around his neck, before she crossed her arms over her chest and leaned back in her seat next to him. He didn't turn to look at her since he already knew her opinion, and he didn't want to see the disapproval on her face.

"I don't agree." There was anger in Sabrina's voice. "That's like saying oppression is okay because it maintains order. If there's a way to rectify wrongs committed against people, it should be explored. But I agree with you that they shouldn't have been made to mate in the first place. Then there wouldn't have been an issue. A mating founded on love will be strengthened by the bond, and the couple won't want to be separated ever again. But I believe the opposite is also true. A forced bond will lead to resentment that will only grow with time and affect everyone around them."

Henry frowned as he recalled his mother's happy voice on the phone. It was like she had been given a second chance at life. He hadn't really thought about it at the time, but her voice and energy could have been that of a much younger woman.

Was he wrong to think that all mating bonds were sacred and should be preserved for the greater good of all shifters? Or was it a lie he had told himself to try to justify his mother's obvious unhappiness?

It hadn't really mattered that much before, since nothing could have changed the established bond. But if people found out what had happened to his mother the day before, there might be people lining up to have their bonds broken. Most couples were happily mated, and for them it would be a tragedy if something happened to destroy their bond. But for those who wanted out of an unhappy mating, Amber might actually turn out to be a hero.

Henry shuddered at how this whole situation could turn into a nightmare scenario. He needed to speak to his mother. She had to keep quiet about what had happened. At least until they could decide how to handle the possible uproar. His mother might not be the only one who had had her bond broken by Amber, but she was the only one known to them.

"Amber is staying not far from your parents' lands." Leith's voice brought Henry out of his head. "If your mother is still there, it might be a good idea to go and talk to her first. It would be valuable to understand how Amber managed to destroy the bond."

Henry nodded, even though Leith couldn't see him. "Yes, I would like to talk to my mother for various reasons, but I'm not entirely sure she's still there. She might be on her way to Inverness by now. I'll find out."

He pulled his phone out of his pocket and placed the call to his mother. It rang until it went to voicemail. He tried again, but the same thing happened.

Frowning, Henry stared down at his phone. The fact that she didn't answer didn't have to mean anything. She might be busy packing, or perhaps she was already on the road and didn't want to talk on the phone while she was driving.

"She's not answering her phone right now." Henry stared at the blanket separating him and Eleanor from the people in the front seat. "But I think it would be a good idea to go there anyway. Even if my mother has already left, my father might have some useful information."

"Okay. Then we'll head there first before we meet up with the others. Sabrina, will you tell the others what we are planning?"

"Yes, I'll call Julianne. She can pass the message on to everyone else."

CHAPTER 24

Eleanor

Eleanor glanced at Henry. He was staring straight ahead, but his focus wasn't on what was in front of his face. It was obvious that this whole situation was difficult for him, and that his parents' less-than-amicable relationship had had a significant impact on him from when he was young.

It was a wonder he had turned out such a kind and caring man at all. That kind of bitterness and resentment could destroy someone. But if anything, it seemed to have turned Henry into a better man, even though he still maintained that mating bonds shouldn't be broken under any circumstances.

She could understand his point of view, even if she didn't agree. A lot of decisions in this world were made for the greater good at the cost of a few individuals' lives. And unfortunately, that was how it had to be sometimes. But she didn't think this was one of those cases.

Correcting old wrongs might actually improve shifter society rather than destroy it. Tearing down old bridges built on rocky foundations and rebuilding on robust supports might help mend old grievances and strengthen the shifter community.

But she had a feeling it was a little early to try to convince Henry of that. She was going to wait until he had spoken to his mother. Because if his mom was as happy about this change as Henry had led Eleanor to believe, it might help sway him.

"I think I need some sleep." Henry's voice was almost mechanical in its deadness, making her study his features. His face was expressionless, and his eyes closed as soon as he leaned his head back against the headrest.

She reached out and put a hand on his thigh, wanting to have some kind of connection to him, even though he seemed to have shut her out. But he made no move to take her hand or cover it with his. In fact, he didn't even seem to notice she was touching him.

It was only about half an hour since he had made her come so hard she had lost the ability to stand, but now there seemed to be an impenetrable wall between them. Something had shifted in him and between them, and she couldn't help worrying that the wall was there to stay.

∞∞∞∞

The sun had already been up for a long time when Leith stopped the car and turned off the engine. As a vampire, Eleanor had a built-in sensor telling her if the sun was up or about to crest the horizon, but she didn't need it to know that the sun was shining. The black plastic and blankets were doing an excellent job of protecting her, but she could still see the glow of light through the material.

Henry had slept or pretended to sleep for most of the three hours they had been on the road. He might not have had much time to sleep in the last few days, but she suspected the main reason his eyes were closed was to avoid talking to her.

Eleanor bit her bottom lip to try to contain the ache in her chest. The tears that filled her eyes were threatening to spill down her cheeks, and she kept her head turned away from him just in case they did. She hadn't expected him to proclaim his undying love for her, but she had expected more of his affection than this after seeing his grin when she had told him she didn't know how to break the bond between them.

"Well, we have finally arrived." There was a smile in Leith's voice. "I am afraid you two lovebirds will have to tear yourself away from each other for a little while. I have parked with your side of the vehicle facing away from the sun, Henry, so you will be able to get out without hurting your girlfriend."

Lovebirds. Eleanor's whole body tensed. Nothing could be further from the truth. They hadn't touched or even shared a look in hours.

"Good. Thank you, Leith." Henry's voice lacked any kind of emotion. "I'll have someone guard the car to make sure you're safe." His statement was obviously directed at her, but she couldn't look at him. And without touching her or saying another word, he opened the door and got out.

The door shut behind him, and she had never felt so abandoned in her life. Fisting her hands so hard her nails dug into her palms, she tried to prevent her tears from falling, but it was like fighting the tide. They flowed down her cheeks like a dam had broken.

She heard Leith and Sabrina get out of the car and close the doors behind them, which left her alone with what felt like a hole in her chest instead of a heart. If only she could have left and gotten out of there. It was what she wanted.

Stupid woman. Henry has just had a massive shock and needs time to process. Get a grip.

She took a deep breath and tried to listen to the rational part of her mind. But it was hard to ignore the pain in her chest, and the deep craving inside her for Henry's affection and approval.

Only hours had passed since she had been dead set against giving in to Henry. But after learning of their bond, everything had changed, and she had let things happen that shouldn't have. That was obvious now through the clear lens of hindsight. If she had stood her ground, she wouldn't have been hurt. Or at least the reason for her pain would be different.

CHAPTER 25

Henry

Henry stared at his mother after introductions had been made. She had sounded younger on the phone, but he hadn't expected her to look younger as well. But she did. She looked younger than he remembered. Perhaps it had something to do with not seeing her for several years, but he didn't think that was the only reason.

His mother had always been considered a beautiful woman, but now she practically radiated happiness and excitement, which enhanced her appearance. Her skin glowed and showed off all her freckles, and her long wavy red hair bounced with every step like it was jumping with joy.

They had been lucky to catch her still on pack lands. She had just finished packing and was about to start loading up the car when they arrived and interrupted her progress, which was accompanied by

Henry's father's angry protests.

Henry's mother turned to them after they had all entered the living room. "Please have a seat. Oh, Henry, it's so nice to see you again. It's been so long since you were here. And you never invited us to visit, so…" She closed the distance to him and pulled him into a tight hug, surprising him.

He hugged her back, although not with as much enthusiasm. Henry couldn't remember the last time he had hugged his mother. They had never been close. Or at least not since he as a kid first sensed the falseness of his parents' relationship.

They stepped away from each other, and Henry took a seat in a chair. It felt safer somehow than taking a seat on the couch, where one of his parents might end up sitting next to him.

Leith and Sabrina sat down on the couch, and Henry's father took up a position by the door, looking like a thundercloud. It was one of his father's regular expressions, so it was nothing unusual or alarming about it. Except that Henry knew the reason this time.

"As you've probably understood by now, this isn't a social call." Henry kept his eyes on his mother. "We need to know more about what happened when Amber showed up. What exactly did she say and do, and more importantly, did she give you a choice?"

His mother sighed, but there was a small smile on her face. "The woman just showed up and rang the bell. I was the one who answered since your father was still busy in the office. She took one look at me before she put her hand on my shoulder. After that everything went black. When I came to, still on my feet mind you, she was standing there, grinning at me like she had just won the lottery or something."

Henry frowned. "And that was it? The bond was gone just like that? Do you know how long you were out?"

Henry's father growled, and his mother's smile widened. "I didn't realize what had happened at first. Before I could say anything, she told me her name and that I was free to go. I had no idea what she meant by that, and I found it rather rude of her to show up on my doorstep and make me black out for a minute. But when I started telling her that, she just waved her hand like it didn't matter and walked off."

Sabrina leaned forward in her seat. "When did you realize what had happened?"

"Not until Martin came storming out of the office, looking like someone had just died." His mother glanced at his father before looking at Sabrina. "It took me a minute to realize that I didn't sense what he was feeling. And that's when I understood the expression on his face. He had thought something happened to me since he lost the connection."

"And now it's time to rectify that." Henry's father stalked toward his mother with a sneer on his face.

His mother's laughter brought Henry's eyes back to her face. "Not in a million years, Martin. I've given you years of my life and two fantastic children. But now I've been given the gift of freedom, and I'll die before I give that up. You have got all you're ever going to get from me."

All the anger drained from the man's face, and his shoulders sagged. His father suddenly looked decades older. Lines that Henry had never noticed before seemed to carve through the man's face. And the difference in age between his father and mother was suddenly so stark, making them look like they were centuries apart when the real age difference was about fifty years.

His mother had just turned twenty when she had been forced to mate his father, a man of sixty-nine. Considering the lifespan of shifters, it wasn't unusual to mate at around seventy or even later, but fifty years difference in life experience was still considered unfavorable. It didn't have to be an issue, but for his parents it had been.

"Louisa, please reconsider." Henry's father sank to his knees next to her chair. "What do you think will happen to shifter society when they realize mating bonds can be broken? Destruction and chaos will happen, and you know it."

Shock reverberated through Henry and made his body jerk like he had just touched a high-voltage source. Hearing his own words spoken by his father made his mind spin with disbelief and horror.

Henry had always considered himself modern and forward-thinking, taking into account both the individual and the big picture in his decisions. His focus had been on what was best for shifters living in a modern society, and breaking with old customs that didn't fit with the current shifter lifestyle and needs had been part of that.

Except he seemed to be as trapped in the old ways as his father was. Henry hadn't made a clean break with old customs and beliefs like he had thought. When faced with something new that could affect shifters forever, he had automatically rejected it and claimed that the old ways were the right ones.

But what if this was something that could be used for the greater good if used correctly? What if it could serve to correct wrongs committed in the past and that were still being committed in some shifter groups? What if Eleanor and Sabrina were right?

Sabrina and Leith asked a few more questions, but Henry struggled to pay attention. He felt like the ground he walked on and trusted had shifted, and he could no longer see the obstacles in his path. Stumbling was inevitable, and he didn't know how far he would fall or how severe the damage would be.

One fact remained, though. Amber needed to be stopped. There might be those who wanted and would benefit from having their mating bond broken, but there were a lot more shifters who didn't and who would do anything to prevent that from happening. And those who had found their true mate were at the top of that list.

Henry followed Leith and Sabrina out of the house. His parents were left arguing in the living room, neither of them ready to give up, but Henry already knew his mother would never agree to mate his father again even if it was possible. She would leave and go somewhere else, and he doubted she would ever go back to even visit the place that held memories of a man and a life she never wanted.

It wasn't until Henry saw the blackened windows of the car that guilt slammed into him. He had barely exchanged a word with Eleanor since they left Leith's house before dawn. In fact, he had pretended to sleep to avoid talking to her. It was despicable behavior, but he hadn't known what else to do.

How did he explain to a woman who had just taken

his cock in her mouth and given him a mind-blowing orgasm that he regretted it? Or that wasn't correct. He couldn't regret it no matter how hard he tried, but he still knew that it could never happen again, and it was time for them to go their separate ways. There was only one path for him, and that was the path that led to his true mate.

"Leith and Sabrina, can you please give me a few minutes to talk to Eleanor alone?"

Sabrina frowned when she turned to look at him, but Leith's face was expressionless.

"Of course." Leith gave him a slow nod. "I will call Trevor and ask where they are and what is happening. I have not heard anything from any of the others, and I am not sure whether to take that as a good sign or a bad one."

Henry gave a sharp nod before he strode over to the car and opened the door to the back seat. He got in while looking away, not able to meet Eleanor's gaze yet. After closing the door, he took a deep breath to steady his voice. "Eleanor, I…"

His voice died when he turned his head to see that she wasn't there. There was no one in the back seat with him. He quickly turned to check the back of the vehicle, but she wasn't there either.

Dread filled his veins with ice when he noticed the blanket between the front and the back seats was missing. He should have noticed it at once, since the sun was streaming into the back seat. But he had been too preoccupied with what he was about to tell her.

CHAPTER 26

Henry

Henry held his breath as he scanned every surface in the car, but there was no sign of any excessive dust or ash, or any burn marks that would have led him to the inevitable conclusion that Eleanor was dead.

"You fucking idiot," he whispered as he closed his eyes. Pulling in a deep breath, he did what he should have done as soon as he discovered her gone—let the bond between them tell him where she was.

Relief flooded him and clogged up his throat when he sensed her location. Eleanor was less than a mile away due south. She was on the move, but her speed was low. It shouldn't take him long to find her. She must be using the missing blanket to protect herself from the sun.

Smiling, he reached for the door handle but stopped himself when he realized the implications of what had happened. Eleanor would never have ventured out into the sun without a good reason. And that reason was that he had hurt her. She was risking the sun's deadly rays to get away from him.

Henry hunched forward and let his head hang in defeat. It felt like whatever he chose to do next would just make this worse. He couldn't in good conscience let her run around in the middle of the day with only a blanket for protection. No matter if she found shelter somewhere, she might be at risk if someone found her. Her last encounter with Amber had proven that.

But him showing up to rescue her like some damsel in distress might not go down too well, considering how he had treated her. It was a *damned if you do and damned if you don't* situation, but he was going to go with the damned if you do option and hope that she would allow him to protect her at least until the sun went down.

After stepping out of the vehicle, he moved over to Leith and Sabrina. "Eleanor is gone, and I need to go pick her up."

The blond woman's eyes widened. "She's gone? But the sun is up. Are you sure she's not…" Sabrina frowned before she looked away.

"She's not dead." Henry swallowed. "She took one of the blankets from the car, and she's about a mile south of here by now. Let's go and I'll tell you when to stop so I can go get her."

Leith cocked his head as he stared at Henry. "And how do you know her exact location? You seem awfully sure where she is and where she is heading."

"I am." He sighed. "We are bonded."

Sabrina gasped.

Henry quickly shook his head at her obvious

misconception. "Not mated but bonded in a vampire way. Eleanor doesn't know exactly how or why it happened, since it's not a common occurrence. But the bond allows me to know exactly where she is at all times, like a built-in GPS if you will, and this is one of the times I'm happy about that."

"Okay." Leith gave a short nod before he took Sabrina's hand in his and gently tugged her toward the car.

As soon as they were on the road, Henry broke the silence. "I...don't know if she'll actually want to come with me. She's running because of me, because of what I did to her. I turned away from her almost as soon as we got into this car, but instead of explaining why I did that, I pretended to sleep." He paused, expecting some kind of outcry from the front seat, but there was nothing.

The uncomfortable silence pressed in on him from all sides, until he couldn't take it anymore and his words rushed out like a waterfall. "I need to find my true mate, since I don't want to end up like my parents. Being with Eleanor will only distract me from my real goal. I should never have given in to my lust for her in the first place. It was stupid and wrong. But now I've hurt her, and that's unacceptable. I'm an asshole." He let his eyes fall shut and leaned his head back against the headrest to receive the inevitable scolding.

Except it didn't happen. And before long they were close to Eleanor's location. "Leith, please pull over here. I'll go talk to her. You don't have to come along."

Henry exited the car before it had even come to a

full stop and hurried across a small field to an old stone cottage with a section of its roof missing. Eleanor was in there. He could feel it. But how she would receive him had yet to be determined.

The door was hanging ajar from one hinge, but the vegetation taking over the building was keeping it in place and preventing it from falling off entirely. "Eleanor? Please don't be alarmed. It's just me, Henry."

He squeezed through the gap before coming to a stop inside the cottage. The light was streaming in through the damaged roof, but it still took him two tries to see the black blanket in the corner, hidden behind a small tree and other plants that had found the neglected building a nice place to live.

"Please leave, Henry. I'll be fine here until dark and then I'll be on my way." There was pain in her voice, and it stabbed into his heart like thousands of tiny needles, making him wince.

"And where are you planning to go?" He tried to keep his tone light, but instead it sounded strained.

"I don't know yet." Her voice was so soft he barely made out the words.

He frowned. "Aren't you forgetting something?"

Silence reigned for several seconds before she sighed so heavily it made him smile. Not because it was funny but because he knew she had given up her plans of running and would come with him back to the car.

Henry pressed his lips together to stop the grin that wanted to split his face in half. But with the way his heart was pounding with joy in his chest it was impossible to fight it.

After pushing through the vegetation, he knelt next to the silent form hidden underneath the blanket. "I'm so sorry, Eleanor. I shouldn't have shut you out like that. The talk about my parents and the prospect of seeing them again and witnessing their broken relationship, it just…"

He had to swallow down the bile in his throat before he could continue. "It reminded me of how important it is to mate the right person." *And the right person for me can't be you, no matter how much I want it to be right now.*

He couldn't tell her that, though. It was too blunt, and truthfully, he wasn't even sure he could utter the words without choking on them. Her running had made him understand that she cared more about him than he had thought, but it also made him realize that he couldn't face the reality of being without her. At least not yet. Whether it was the vampire bond talking or not didn't really matter.

Pulling in a deep breath, he made a decision. Until they could find a way to break the bond tying them to each other, he was going to focus on Eleanor and enjoy the time they had together. Any thoughts of the future would have to wait. He could pick those up again as soon as the bond to Eleanor was removed.

His heart squeezed painfully at what breaking that bond would mean, but he pushed that thought to the back of his mind. Perhaps it would take a day or a week to find the information they needed to break the bond, and until then he would live and feel and not worry about the future. There would be time enough to search for his mate afterward. A week wouldn't make any difference in the long run.

The blanket moved, and Eleanor rose to her feet. "Okay. Please help me back to the car."

The dejection in her voice made Henry frown, and without thinking, he rose and threw his arms around her, pulling her tightly to his chest. "Please let me make it up to you. For being an asshole and treating you like shit. Just tell me what to do. I can't promise you forever, but I can promise you right now. I really want to spend time with you, get to know you, just…be with you. But if you don't want that, I'll stay away. I won't push you into accepting a short fling with me if that's not something you want."

CHAPTER 27

Eleanor

Eleanor squeezed her eyes shut at his words. She wanted what he'd suggested, and a fling was all she could ever have with him anyway. She shouldn't agree to it, considering her maker would disapprove, but since they already had a bond, a temporary relationship wouldn't put Henry in any more danger than he already was. And she would be right there to protect him if all hell broke loose.

It was going to hurt like hell to leave him at the end of it, though. She had tried to keep her feelings for him from growing into something more, but it had been doomed from the start. It was almost like he was made for her—he was that perfect. And if she had been given an option to choose one thing she wanted above all else, she would have chosen Henry and gladly given up her immortality and everything else she had to have his love and devotion for even a short time.

"I want that." Her voice was so low she didn't expect him to have heard her, but before she could repeat her words, he tightened his hold on her.

"Thank you." There was a smile in his voice. Then he took her head in his hands and kissed her forehead through the blanket. "Come. I'll take you back to the car."

Eleanor let him guide her out of the cottage. She didn't venture outside during the day often, but she could if she was careful and covered herself properly. The difficult part was to keep an eye on where she was going while protecting her eyes from direct sunlight and any reflection of the sun's rays. She could wear sunglasses, although they weren't perfect, but she hadn't found any in Leith's car.

As soon as they had squeezed past the damaged door, Henry grabbed her and swung her into his arms, startling her and making her laugh.

"You don't have to carry me. I can walk, you know."

He chuckled. "I know, but I feel like carrying you right now, okay? Besides, it will take us less time to get back to the car this way, and I don't have to worry about you stumbling and losing the blanket."

Warmth spread through her chest and made her smile. "Thank you." She had no objections to being in Henry's strong arms. In fact, she was going to make sure to enjoy every second she spent with him, because no matter how long it lasted, it wouldn't be long enough.

He held her securely while striding across what felt like even ground. She should have known he would come after her, and thinking about it, she felt a little embarrassed that she had run away in the first place. But there was something about Henry that made her act more on impulse than she had ever done before. And she knew what it was. She had never felt about anyone the way she felt about Henry. No one had ever mattered to her like he did.

"Thank you, Leith."

Henry's words to Leith were the only warning she got before he deposited her on what she assumed was the back seat of the car. "I'll get in on the other side. Don't remove the blanket yet, okay?"

"I won't." Eleanor frowned, wondering why he would even tell her that. She was wearing the blanket that had been used as a barrier for the sun between the back seat and the front of the vehicle. Removing it would leave her basking in the sun, and that wasn't something she had any intention of ever doing again.

Henry got in next to her and closed the door behind him. "You can remove the blanket now. Leith and Sabrina have covered the access to the front seats with black plastic. It's safe."

"Oh, okay." She chuckled. Eleanor carefully removed the blanket before turning to look at Henry.

His lips stretched into a smile when she met his gaze, and the warmth in his hazel eyes made her chest expand with longing. If she didn't know better, she would have called his gaze loving, but she *did* know better and nurturing that kind of hope would only come back to bite her later. She would take all the attention he was willing to give her, but she wouldn't engage in any hopes or wishes for the future. Because there was no future for her and Henry together.

His hand clasped hers, and she smiled back at him while taking in every detail of his face to commit to memory for when she no longer had access to him. Perhaps one day she would meet someone like him that could be hers for real. It was unlikely, but a woman could dream.

"What's wrong?" His brows pushed together as he studied her face.

Eleanor hadn't even realized her smile had died in response to her thoughts. "Just thinking. And I guess...worrying. We don't know what will happen next with Amber." It was the truth, just not what she had been thinking about right then.

Giving her a reassuring smile, Henry put his arm around her shoulders and tucked her against him. "True. But we'll find a way to stop her." He kissed her forehead, a gesture that felt more like a sign of love than of lust.

Leith cleared his throat. "I talked to Trevor. They have checked out the place where Amber was staying, but it is deserted. She seems to have left with no plan to return. Callum and Vamika are trying to track her. We have agreed to meet them in Wick to decide what to do next. And get something to eat."

"Well, I'm not really surprised." Henry's hand curved around Eleanor's neck, gently caressing her skin. "It took us a while to get here, and for all we know, Amber was only here to demonstrate what she is capable of and get our attention. And she succeeded. Let's hope she didn't just do this to get us out of the way to carry out something more sinister somewhere else."

The inside of the car was quiet for several seconds

before Sabrina spoke. "That's a good point, and one we should've considered. But we need the numbers when facing off with Amber. She's too powerful for a couple of people to face alone. Although, I don't know what Aidan can do. Perhaps he can kill her without even breaking a sweat."

"I doubt it." There was a frown in Leith's voice. "Aidan is powerful, but not invincible. He is immortal in the sense that he does not age, but like every other being, there are ways to kill him. But whether Amber is powerful enough to pose a threat to him I honestly do not know."

Henry sucked in a breath when Eleanor put her hand underneath his shirt and smoothed it up his stomach. His abs bunched under her palm in reaction to her touch, and his hand around her neck tightened. Just the feel of his smooth naked skin was enough to heat her body.

He had promised her right now but how long that would be was impossible to say, which meant she had to make the most of the time she had with him. And if that time was in the back seat of this car, then so be it.

Leith and Sabrina were still talking but Eleanor couldn't focus on their words anymore. Henry's closeness was occupying all her senses, and all she wanted to do was drown herself in everything that was him.

"Eleanor." He spoke her name in a low whisper, but it was still filled with so much desire her channel clenched.

Fighting a smile, she pinched his nipple. His whole body jerked in response, making her chuckle.

A low growl was the only warning she got before

he grabbed her chin and raised her face to his. Hard lips crashed against hers before his tongue delved into her mouth like he owned it.

She whimpered as he took possession of her mouth, filling her whole body with a need so strong it blocked out all thoughts. Clinging to him, she kissed him back with everything she had, like it was the last time she would ever get to do this. And who knew, perhaps it was.

Strong hands grabbed her hips and lifted her off the seat, and she soon found herself on Henry's lap with her clit tightly pressed against his erection.

She shuddered at how good it felt to be the sole focus of his attention. And it wasn't just the heat building in her lower belly, but his possessive kiss and his tight embrace made her feel like she meant something more than just a short fling.

Eleanor couldn't help being jealous of the woman who ended up being his mate. She hoped the lucky bitch knew how amazing he was and took care of him the way he deserved. Because otherwise Eleanor would have to intervene.

Except she couldn't, of course. True mates were forever and killing one would kill the other. The only consolation was that true mates were supposed to be perfect for each other, so the likelihood of Henry's mate hurting him was low.

Henry ripped his lips from hers before pressing them to her ear. His voice was barely a whisper when he spoke. "If we weren't stuck in this car with other people, I would rip your clothes off and fuck you like my life depended on it. But I can promise you that as soon as we have some time alone together, I will do exactly that."

Wetness pooled between her legs, and a shiver ran along her spine from her neck to her tailbone. "I…can't wait."

Need took hold of her body, and she ground her aching clit against the thick steel bar in his pants. She needed release more than her next breath, and she couldn't care less if Leith and Sabrina realized what was going on.

"I'm sorry," he whispered as his grip on her hips tightened, and he pushed her back until the sweet friction between them was lost.

She couldn't help the whine that escaped her. Her clit was throbbing, and she couldn't even close her legs to alleviate some of the insistent need while straddling his legs.

Eleanor pulled in a deep breath to try to quell some of her desperate desire. But it was like pouring a bucket of water on a raging barn fire—no detectable effect whatsoever. Her need was like a fire in her veins being fed by just enough gasoline to keep it burning but not enough to let it grow.

"Look at me." Henry's hand cupped her chin.

Her eyes flew open, and she met his gaze. She hadn't even realized her eyes were closed until that moment.

Henry's eyes were almost black with desire. His lips stretched into a grin, and he put his index finger across his lips, signaling for her to stay quiet.

Eleanor didn't have time to wonder what he was up to before his hand disappeared down into her leggings and brushed across her clit through the moist material of her panties. Taken by surprise, she gasped at the tendrils of pleasure that rushed through her body.

Shaking his head slowly, Henry narrowed his eyes at her.

Fuck. She was supposed to be quiet, but she hadn't expected him to touch her like that after pushing her away. Biting down on her bottom lip, she nodded.

When he smiled and brushed his finger over her clit again, she shuddered and bit down harder on her lip to keep from making any noise.

It felt so good to have him caress her swollen nub, but she needed more. His touch was too gentle and was going to drive her crazy before long. Staring into his eyes, she tilted her hips forward to try to push into his touch, but instead of obliging her, he grinned and lifted his hand to caress up her belly.

CHAPTER 28

Eleanor

Eleanor was just getting ready to shout at Henry for teasing her, when his hand suddenly dove into her panties, making her bite down so hard on her lip she tasted blood. His middle finger slid through her wet folds before sinking into her body.

Oh, God yes. Please make me explode. Squeezing her eyes closed, she focused on staying silent while her body was screaming for release.

"Look at me." His palm pressed against her clit.

Rocking against his hand, she forced her eyes open and met his gaze again. Focusing was difficult with how turned on she was, but there was no mistaking the wicked grin on his face, telling her he knew exactly how desperate she was for that orgasm he was keeping out of her reach.

Please. Eleanor mouthed the word. She wasn't above begging if it would get her what she wanted.

His grin softened, and he added another digit before pumping them into her pussy. After a few languid thrusts of his fingers, his thumb found her clit and rubbed.

It was hard to keep her gaze on his when all she wanted was to lose herself in the amazing sensations he was creating. She was so close she could practically taste her orgasm.

Henry suddenly leaned in and nipped her shoulder, and pleasure exploded through her and sent her soaring among the clouds.

Eleanor didn't know how long she wallowed in a haze of pleasure before she finally blinked her eyes open. Her head was resting against Henry's shoulder, and his arms were wrapped around her. She felt so safe and treasured in his arms that she could almost forget they weren't in a real relationship.

Pushing those thoughts away, she silently berated herself for letting thoughts like that taint the time they had together. There would be time enough for regrets and anguish later. Now was the time to make memories she could revisit forever.

Henry laid his cheek against the top of her head, and the sweetness of the gesture made her smile. This man had a gorgeous exterior, but he was just as beautiful on the inside. And that was surprising considering the childhood he must have had with a mother who had been forced to mate someone she didn't want. It was hard to imagine the horror of that scenario.

Something vibrated against Eleanor's inner thigh, and she lifted her head from Henry's shoulder to stare at him. It wasn't until he reached into his pocket and pulled out his phone that she realized what the vibration was.

She chuckled at her own confusion, and Henry smiled at her when he answered the call.

"Nes. So you've finally decided to talk to your brother. I guess you've heard the news about mom and dad then."

There was a pause before Henry's sister answered. "Yes. Is it true or has mom finally gone crazy?"

Eleanor wasn't sure she should be listening in on Henry's conversation with his sister, but she was sitting so close it was impossible not to hear what the woman was saying. And Henry still had one arm wrapped around Eleanor, making it clear he wasn't about to let her go.

"It's true." Henry's brows furrowed.

"But how?" The disbelief in the woman's voice was loud and clear. "Mom mentioned something about a woman doing this to her, but how can anyone do anything to a mating bond? It's supposed to be unbreakable. Has that been another shifter lie to make us conform to the traditions that serve men and shackle women?"

Henry sighed. "Don't you think it would have been a bit difficult to keep something like that a secret? Someone would have found out at some stage if mating bonds could be broken that easily."

Nes huffed. "Perhaps. But I reserve my right to be skeptical of all shifter traditions. The majority of them seem to be beneficial to men and not to women. But it doesn't really matter to me anymore. I'm never going to be anyone's mate anyway."

"I know. You've told me countless times." Henry's

jaw tensed. "This is the work of a witch, though. One who is specifically targeting shifters with the intention to hurt them and kill them."

A chuckle sounded through the phone. "A witch? Is that the story mom is spreading for her miraculous escape? Jeez, I was right. She *is* going crazy."

"I wish it was that simple." Henry leaned his head back against the headrest. "Witches exist, Nes. Both good ones and bad ones, and the one who destroyed our parents' mating bond is a truly evil one. She has already killed several shifters to siphon their power during mating. Her goal is to eradicate us all."

Twenty seconds went by before Nes said anything. "You are serious. And... Oh shit. You mean the killings that have been all over the media lately, that's her?"

"Yes, that's her." Closing his eyes, Henry tightened his hold on Eleanor. "Amber is growing more powerful with everyone she kills. Or at least that's our theory. We haven't really been able to confirm that yet. But her expressed goal is to kill us all."

"How do you know this? Have you met her?" There was disbelief in Nes's voice.

"Yes, unfortunately I've had that displeasure." Henry opened his eyes and met Eleanor's gaze. "And now I'm working with some friends to try to destroy her. Amber won't stop what she's doing, so we have no choice but to kill her. And hopefully, we'll be able to do that before humans realize we exist. Where are you staying at the moment?"

"In Wick. I've been living here for a couple of years now, running a restaurant."

"Really?" Henry's eyes widened in astonishment. "I

thought you would have ventured further away from home. You seemed dead set against living in Scotland at all the last time we spoke. What happened?"

"I lived in London for a while. But then…" Nes's heavy sigh was audible through the phone. "I guess I'm a small-town girl. So I moved to Wick, but I didn't tell anyone from the pack, and so far I've been able to stay off their radar."

"Well, are you open?" Henry chuckled. "I mean your restaurant. Is it open?"

"We're just about to open. Why are you asking? Are you in the area?" Eleanor could practically hear the frown in Nes's voice.

"Yes, we're heading toward Wick as we speak. Do you have room for fifteen, no sixteen people for a late lunch?" Henry's smile stretched wide.

Eleanor's whole body tensed at the prospect of meeting Henry's sister. Eleanor was just a fling, so what would happen when they got there? Would Henry acknowledge her at all, or would he pretend there was nothing between them? The thought that he might keep her at a distance when they met his sister sent a stab of pain through her unbeating heart.

Eleanor had been trying to push the knowledge that this wasn't a permanent arrangement between them to the back of her mind. But meeting Henry's sister might change their agreement to have a temporary fling a bit earlier than she had hoped. She had hope to get a few days with him at the very least, but it didn't seem like that would be possible.

"I'll see you soon then." Henry was smiling when he ended the call, but his smile soon died when he looked at her. "What's wrong? Are you all right?"

She should have made sure to hide her emotions, but the whole situation had taken her by surprise, and the pain was too prominent to be easily concealed. "I'm... It's nothing."

Eleanor looked away and tried to move off his lap, but Henry tightened his arm around her. She was strong and could have gotten out of his grip if she really wanted to, but that would have proven to him that what she was feeling was more than nothing.

"Eleanor, look at me." He grabbed her chin and gently turned her head to face him. His expression was unreadable when their gazes met.

Her stomach twisted into a hard knot when all her hope died. Their fling was already over even before it had really started. Tears pricked her eyes, and she bit her bottom lip to try to contain them. The last thing she wanted was to show him how much it hurt when he let her go.

"I look forward to introducing you to my sister."

Eleanor blinked several times to try to make sense of what he had just said. She had been preparing to pretend that his rejection was understandable and that she didn't expect him to introduce her to his sister as anything other than an acquaintance. But what did he mean exactly? What kind of introduction was he talking about?

Henry's brows pushed together as he studied her face. "Or if you're not comfortable with Nes knowing about our arrangement, I'll just introduce you the same as I will everyone else."

Something fluttered in her stomach, and her lips stretched into a wide smile. He hadn't intended to hide who she was from his sister. And she probably shouldn't have expected anything else from a man who valued honesty. *I swear I'm turning into a mental case. But then perhaps that's what love does to people.* She had never let herself love anyone before for obvious reasons, but she knew that was what she felt about Henry.

Eleanor put her hand on his cheek, letting his stubble prick her fingers. "No. Please be honest with your sister. I'd like to be by your side while I can."

"Good." He gave her a small smile before his gaze dipped to her mouth. "Then that's settled."

He closed the distance between them and brushed his lips over hers once, before he took possession of her mouth again. And somehow he seemed to be able to take possession of her mind as well because she was soon lost to his kisses.

CHAPTER 29

Henry

"Henry." Leith's voice somehow penetrated the lust clogging up his brain. "What is the name of your sister's restaurant? From your conversation with her I gather that is where we are going to eat."

Henry reluctantly pulled away from Eleanor. The woman had a way of making him forget everything else when he was with her. But thankfully, he seemed to have an effect on her as well, so at least he wasn't the only one prone to lose his sense of time and place when they were together.

He doubted she was as affected as he was, though. For the first time in his life, Henry was considering canceling his search for his true mate in favor of mating another woman. But Eleanor might not want that. She was attracted to him and did care about him to a certain degree, but that didn't mean she cared enough to want to spend forever with him.

"The Wolf and Prey. I'm surprised she didn't call the restaurant werewolf or wolf shifter, but I guess that has something to do with her wanting to stay under the pack's radar." Henry smirked at the sight of Eleanor's swollen lips. He liked the clear evidence of their kissing, and he couldn't help hoping her lips would stay like that until everyone realized what they had been doing. But unfortunately, her vampire healing would restore her lips to normal within a minute or two.

Leith chuckled, which was a rare sound coming from him, but one Henry had heard more often since the man found his true mate. "A fitting name for a shifter-owned establishment. I look forward to meeting your sister again. I do not believe I have seen her since you were children."

Henry nodded until he remembered that Leith couldn't see him. "Well, I believe she hasn't changed much. It seems she's still as stubborn as ever."

Eleanor lifted an eyebrow at him. "So, it runs in the family then?"

Laughter sounded from the front of the car.

Henry lifted an eyebrow right back at her. "Yes, and apparently it's contagious because it seems to have been spreading."

Eleanor laughed, and more laughter sounded from the front. "I'll remember that when I need someone to blame it on. At least it's not my fault I'm stubborn."

Henry winked at her before he clasped her head in his hands and gave her a hard kiss. "Nice to have someone to blame, isn't it?" Then he grabbed her hips and lifted her off his lap and placed her on the seat beside him.

He adjusted his rock-hard cock in his pants. The poor thing must have an imprint of his zipper permanently etched into it by now. But there was nothing he could do about that. Getting any kind of relief would have to wait until after they had eaten, but hopefully his erection would realize it would be a long wait and give up long before then.

But that would only happen if he could get the image of Eleanor's face as she orgasmed out of his head. He wanted to see that again, multiple times, but that would have to wait as well.

A hand palmed his hard shaft, and he groaned before he could stop himself. Even through the fabric of his pants, Eleanor's touch felt amazing.

Grabbing her hand, he shook his head at her.

"Why not?" She frowned at him.

"We're almost there, aren't we, Leith?"

"Yes," Leith confirmed from the front. "Just looking for somewhere to park."

Eleanor pulled her hand away with a sigh. "Later then."

He put his arm around her shoulders and pulled her close before kissing her temple. If he could have come up with a good excuse for not joining the others for lunch, he wouldn't have hesitated. But it was his sister's restaurant, and it would be more than a little strange if he didn't show up. And then there was the fact that he would like to see Nes again and introduce her to Eleanor.

His sister had left the pack before he did, and he hadn't seen her since. They had always been friends, even though they had vastly different opinions about mating and shifter traditions. She had laughed when he told her he planned to find his true mate, since she had no plan of ever taking a mate of her own. A mate to her was synonymous with restrictions and control, not with love and companionship. And he had no trouble understanding why.

The car came to a stop, and Henry picked up the blanket from the floor before turning to look at Eleanor. "Put this on, and I'll carry you to the restaurant."

Eleanor's eyes widened. "Do you really want it to look like you're carrying a dead body around in the middle of the day? I think it might be better if I use my own two feet to get there. Just put your arm around my shoulders and guide me. That way I at least look alive if a bit strange with the blanket covering me."

Henry chuckled. "I don't think people would actually believe you're dead, but even if they did, they would be right."

"Really? Dead person joke?" She glared at him and crossed her arms over her chest, but the corner of her lips twitched with amusement. "And what do you think your sister is going to say when you carry a dead body into her restaurant?"

He laughed. "She'd see the irony. Or would you rather be presented as dead on your feet? Your choice."

"Oh, please." Eleanor rolled her eyes. "Trust me, I've heard all the jokes about dead or dying already. You can't surprise me."

"Are you going to stay here bickering or are you coming to eat with us?" Leith blew out a breath like he was tired of dealing with the kids who had been sitting too long in the back seat together, which according to the parents Henry knew was anything longer than three minutes.

"We'll be out the second I've talked some sense into this stubborn man." Eleanor narrowed her gaze at Henry like she was offering him a challenge.

Sabrina laughed. "Good luck with that. From my experience shifter men are nothing if not stubborn."

Leith chuckled. "I seem to recall a saying about a pot and a kettle, my angel. I wonder which of them is you."

"I have no idea what you're talking about." The sound of Sabrina's laughter softened when the front doors closed.

"If you want to walk, I have no problem with that. I'll guide you and keep you safe." Henry smiled at the gorgeous woman beside him. How he was going to give her up, he couldn't even begin to imagine. But there would be time enough to deal with that later. They would have to find a solution to the vampire bond first, and hopefully that would take a while.

"Thank you." Eleanor grinned at him before pulling the blanket over her head.

He looked her over to make sure she was fully covered, before he opened the door and helped her out of the car. Leith and Sabrina were waiting for them, and Henry signaled for them to lead the way to the restaurant, since he had no idea where it was located.

His sister's restaurant was beautifully situated in one of the old buildings overlooking Wick Harbor. The rest of their large group was already inside when they entered, and his sister and a couple of her staff were busy arranging a long table for them all to fit.

Nes looked the same as she had the last time he saw her. She was as different to him in coloring as he considered possible with the same parents. Her short black hair and dark-blue eyes resembled his grandmother's on his father's side, whereas he looked more like his mother.

His sister looked up and on seeing him, her face split in a bright smile. "Brother. And…" Her gaze fell on the blanket still covering Eleanor before returning to his with one eyebrow raised in question.

"Sis." Henry grinned and led Eleanor away from the door and front windows. "Eleanor, you can remove the blanket now."

The woman by his side pulled the blanket off and brushed her hair back from her face. She shot him a smile before letting her gaze wander around the room until it stopped on Nes. "You must be Henry's sister. I'm pleased to meet you." Eleanor walked forward and extended her hand.

"Likewise." Shaking Eleanor's hand, Nes gave her a wide smile before tilting her head to the side. "Not trying to be rude here, but you're not a shifter. May I ask what you are?"

Eleanor chuckled. "You may. I'm a vampire, or as some people like to call me, dead on my feet." She glanced at Henry over her shoulder before returning her gaze to his sister.

Nes laughed. "Hence the blanket. This summer has been sunnier than usual in Scotland. I guess you're one of the few who doesn't appreciate that."

Smiling, Eleanor nodded. "You could say that, but I don't mind that much either way. I don't venture out much during the day rain or shine. I guess you could call me a night person."

"So, is this my brother's doing then, taking you outside during the day?" His sister narrowed her gaze at him. "He has a penchant for talking people into things they don't want. Things that he considers the only correct way. Isn't that right, brother?"

Eleanor just laughed and shook her head. "No. If it was up to him, I think he would have had me locked up in a windowless room somewhere."

"Good." Nes's eyes widened. "That he wants to protect you I mean. Not that he wants to lock you up."

Chuckling at his sister's flustered look, Henry walked up to her and threw his arms around her. "It's nice to see you again, sis, and great to see that you haven't changed much."

Nes sighed as she leaned into him and wrapped her arms around his waist. "Yes well, that's unfortunate, because I was really hoping I had evolved from where I was."

CHAPTER 30

Gawen

Gawen couldn't take his eyes off the stunning woman, who was Henry's sister. He didn't think he had ever seen anyone more beautiful. Short black hair fashioned in some kind of spiky look that went well with her high cheekbones and her dark considering gaze.

She had greeted them all individually when they arrived, having already been informed that they were her brother's friends. Her smile had been warm and genuine, yet there had been an air of distance like she wanted to keep this professional.

He had tried to catch her gaze ever since they had shaken hands, but she had yet to spare him a second glance. And with her brother's arrival, she was too busy talking to him to notice Gawen.

Swallowing hard, he tore his gaze away from Nes and looked at the other people from their group standing around the room. He was the odd one out, not having a mate or even a potential mate by his side. Except for Aidan, but the enforcer didn't belong to the group.

It wasn't like it was a surprise, though. Gawen was the strange one in the group, the hybrid that didn't fit in anywhere. It wasn't anything new, so he should be used to it by now, but for some reason he kept hoping he would one day find a mate that wanted him just the way he was. With all his strangeness and faults.

"Well, why don't you all take a seat, and I'll get you some menus."

Gawen swung his gaze back to Nes at the sound of her voice, and his breathing ceased when he found her looking straight at him. It only lasted a couple of seconds, but it was enough to make his heart speed up.

He let out a shaky breath when she turned away and walked over to the counter. It was a good thing she hadn't said anything specifically to him or asked him a question, because he didn't think he would have been able to respond at all while caught in the spotlight of her gaze.

Making his way over to the table, he kept glancing her way, but she was too busy doing something behind the counter to look up.

Gawen found a seat between Henry and Julianne. He didn't know anyone in the group well yet, but they had all been very welcoming, and it didn't seem to have anything to do with Henry being his new alpha. The only one who eyed him with suspicion was Bryson, and there was a good reason for that.

But what had surprised Gawen the most was that no one had asked him what he was. People invariably noticed there was something different about him, and they usually proceeded to give him the third degree. But none of these people had. The fact that he was different didn't seem to matter that much to them, which was unusual for shifters. But then they weren't all shifters, but a mixed group of humans, shifters, and a vampire.

Nes started moving around the table, handing each person a menu, and he waited in anticipation for her to reach him. As soon as she had given Henry his menu, Gawen turned to smile at her. She returned his smile, but there was something in her gaze that clearly told him to keep his distance.

She held out the menu, and he gave her a small nod when he accepted it. "Tha…thank you." His embarrassing stutter caused his shoulders to tense, but she didn't seem to notice as she moved to Julianne.

Gawen looked down at the menu in his hand, but the words swirled in front of his eyes as the voices in his head started berating him for his awkward behavior. *You stupid idiot. Why do you even bother trying to get a beautiful woman's attention? What do you have to offer her? Nothing. Exactly nothing. So stop expecting people to like you. Because they never will. You're not worth anything to anyone.*

He fisted the hand that wasn't holding the menu and tried to force his insecurity to the back of his mind. The voices had been there for as long as he could remember, and he wasn't more than ten years old when he realized that telling people about them only caused everyone to pull away from him and look at him with pity and disgust. And he already had enough of that just being who he was. Giving people another reason to hate him was stupid.

"Will you join us for lunch, Nes?"

Henry mentioning his sister's name pulled Gawen out of his head, and he scanned the room until he found Nes standing by the end of the table.

She smiled at her brother. "I don't usually eat with my guests, but I might make an exception for you. You are my favorite brother, after all." Then she turned on her heel and walked away.

"I'd better be, considering I'm your only one," Henry called after her.

Nes laughed as she disappeared through the door to the kitchen.

The sound of her laughter caressed Gawen's skin like luscious velvet and filled his body with a pleasant heat that caused his cock to thicken. Taking a deep breath, he discreetly adjusted his shirt to make sure no one would notice his condition.

The best thing for him to do would be to walk out of the restaurant and wait for the others by the cars. He had never reacted to a woman like this before, not from just the sound of her laughter. And he wasn't sure whether he liked it or not. He preferred to stay in control, and he most assuredly wasn't in control at the moment.

But it would be impossible to explain why he wanted to leave, and Henry might take offense at Gawen leaving, considering it was his sister's restaurant. Insulting the first alpha to ever welcome him into a pack willingly was unacceptable.

The two servers who had been helping Nes set the table earlier came and took their orders. Gawen sincerely hoped Nes had enough help in the kitchen to cook the massive amount of food they ordered.

Shifters, particularly male ones, ate twice that of a human man the same size, but Henry's sister would know that being a wolf herself.

A few minutes later, Nes came back out of the kitchen and headed toward their table with a glass and cutlery in her hands.

"Why don't you sit down between me and Gawen? We can make room for you."

Henry's suggestion made Gawen snap his head around to stare at his alpha, and his already hard cock twitched at the thought of sitting next to the stunning owner of the restaurant.

Everyone on his side of the table started moving their chairs to make room for Nes, and Gawen followed suit. He couldn't very well protest, even though he was feeling both excited and uncomfortable at the thought of having her so close.

Nes sat down next to him and immediately engaged in a conversation with her brother. The tension in Gawen's shoulders gradually eased as Henry asked Nes questions about where she had been staying and what she had been doing since she moved away from their parents' pack, and she seemed to do her best to answer her brother as vaguely as possible.

It didn't take long before Nes took over and started asking questions about Amber and what was going on, and Henry recounted what had happened and how they were trying to stop her.

Their drinks arrived and the conversation paused while the servers made sure everyone received what they had ordered.

"So let me get this straight." Henry's sister swung her gaze around the table. "Three of you ladies are witches? I had no idea witches even existed before Henry told me on the phone earlier."

Most of the people around the table nodded.

Henry chuckled. "I think that is true for most shifters. But to be more precise, we have four people who have magical powers around this table. Gawen can do magic as well."

Henry's statement made Nes turn to look at Gawen with wide eyes, and Gawen's spine stiffened with apprehension.

"Really?" Nes stared at him. "You're a witch as well?" She frowned. "Or I suppose whatever the male counterpart is called."

Gawen shook his head slowly as he found himself drowning in her eyes. "I... No, I... I have magic, but I'm not a warlock."

Tilting her head to the side, she scrutinized his face. "Not a warlock. Okay."

His pulse seemed to hammer in his ears while he kept his gaze on her face, waiting for her to ask what he was. But after a few long seconds, she turned away from him.

"So what is it witches can do exactly?" Nes stared across the table at Sabrina this time. "Can all of you remove a shifter's mating bond? Because if that's the case, I'm surprised my brother wants to spend time with you. He's nothing if not religiously protective of the mating bond."

Henry spoke before Sabrina could say anything. "You make it sound like I'm a fanatic. I'm not, and I'm coming to accept that some bonds might not be worth preserving. We can't allow Amber to continue, though, because destruction of mating bonds is not her ultimate goal. We'll all be dead soon if we let that evil bitch continue on her mission to eradicate us all."

Nes laughed. "Well, it seems you lot have had a positive influence on my brother. He needed to loosen up a little and let traditions be traditions and not the rule for the future. But I would really like to know what witches can do, and not just about mating bonds."

Sabrina smiled. "Different witches have different abilities, but I haven't heard of anyone other than Amber who can destroy a mating bond. Some abilities are destructive, and some are constructive, but that will also depend on the setting and how it is used."

Nes's brows pushed together in thought. "I think I can imagine the destructive part, but what do you mean by constructive in this case?"

"Healing." Sabrina looked at Gawen. "Both Steph and Gawen can heal people's injuries. Gawen healed Fia's fatal wound in a matter of seconds."

Nes snapped her head around to stare at him. "Seconds. That's impressive."

Gawen's chest expanded with her praise, and he gave her a tentative smile.

"And then he immediately asked Fia to be his mate." Bryson's voice was little more than a growl, coming from near one end of the table. "I'm not impressed with that, even though I owe him everything for saving my true mate."

Nes's expression tightened, and her eyes darkened with disapproval, before she looked away.

Gawen had no trouble understanding Nes's reaction. He had never intended to ask Fia to be his mate. But the woman had just saved him from serious injury and sacrificed her own safety, and something about her had told him she was in pain. Not just physical pain but emotional. Asking her to be his mate had felt like something he should do as a repayment of sorts. He had met several women who wanted someone to take care of them, but Fia wasn't one of those. She was stronger than that, and unbeknownst to him at the time, she had a true mate.

"If you'll excuse me. I'll just…" Gawen let the sentence die as he pushed his chair back and got to his feet. He needed some air. The whole room suddenly felt stuffy and like it lacked oxygen. He knew it was all in his head, but that didn't matter. If he didn't get out of there soon, he would suffocate.

Bryson's disapproval hadn't really bothered him before, since Gawen knew where it was coming from. But having Nes's opinion of him destroyed had been like a kick in the nuts.

CHAPTER 31

Eleanor

Eleanor frowned as she watched Gawen hurry out of the restaurant. From the brief glimpse she got of his face he looked distraught, but she wasn't sure why since she didn't have the impression he harbored any deeper feelings for Fia. But perhaps she had misunderstood something. She hadn't spent a lot of time with him and didn't know him well.

She gripped Henry's hand to get his attention before speaking in a low voice. "Is Gawen all right? He looked…devastated."

Henry glanced at the door before turning back to face her. "I don't know, but let's give him a few minutes. If he hasn't come back by then, I'll go look for him."

"Okay." Eleanor nodded. "Perhaps he's fine and just needed some air."

Henry smiled before leaning in and whispering in

her ear. "Do you need something to…eat?"

"No." She chuckled before continuing in a low voice. "And even if I did, I don't think this is the time and place for that. Do you remember how you reacted last time?"

"I do and you're right."

The food started arriving, and before everyone had received what they had ordered, Gawen came back inside and sat down with a neutral expression on his face. Eleanor wasn't fooled by his seemingly relaxed demeanor, though. There was a weariness in his eyes that shouldn't have been there.

The conversation around the table died down when everyone started eating. Eleanor was the only one who wasn't shoving food into her mouth, and she took the opportunity to study the people around the table while sipping her coffee.

All the couples she could see from where she was sitting were so obviously happy together. A smile, a small caress, and a few whispered words. They were all displaying the telltale signs of being in love and unable to stay away from each other.

Apart from Gawen, Nes, Henry, and herself, Aidan was the only one who wasn't happily mated. And from the rumors she had picked up the last time she met him almost three centuries ago, he wasn't allowed to mate. Although she had never been told why, and she wasn't entirely sure that the rumors were true.

The group of enforcers Aidan belonged to was a bit of an enigma. No one knew anything about their history, how old they were or where they came from, but they were all immortal and had extraordinary powers. And they tended to show up whenever there was a serious problem somewhere in the supernatural world.

Julianne rose and headed toward the back of the room before disappearing down a corridor where Eleanor assumed the restrooms were located. She couldn't imagine Duncan would let Julianne out of his sight for anything else. It was like invisible strings tied each of the couples together, since one never ventured far away from the other. There were exceptions, of course, but those just proved the rule.

Eleanor turned her head and studied Henry's profile. She could happily spend hours looking at his face. The purpose of her life had quickly changed over the last few days and was now centered around this man. Around the hope of having a future with him.

Something about him had pulled her to him from the second she first saw him, and she suspected that her attraction to him was the main reason the vampire bond had formed.

Or perhaps it was the mutual attraction between them. Henry had said that he had been attracted to her scent before he had even seen her. Her bite might have instigated the bond, but it hadn't created the attraction. And she suspected the love she was feeling for this man wasn't caused by the bond either. It was all him.

The whole table shook when Duncan suddenly jumped up, causing his chair to fall back and hit the floor with a crack. A millisecond later he was off toward the restrooms, and everyone else got to their feet so fast more chairs fell to the floor, and several of the glasses on the table toppled over, spilling their contents.

Trevor and Leith stormed after Duncan, and Aidan was right behind them.

Henry's hand covered hers and made her realize her fingers had sunk deep into the muscles of his thigh, probably leaving horrible bruises. But he didn't say anything, just gently peeled her hand off his thigh before wrapping his hand around hers.

Swallowing hard, she stared at the entrance to the corridor. Something had happened to Julianne, and there was no doubt who was responsible, but she hoped it wasn't serious. Duncan's reaction wasn't a good sign, though.

"Let me go." The anger in Nes's voice made Eleanor lean back to look at Henry's sister.

"Please don't go after them. You'll get hurt." Gawen had his arms wrapped around Nes, holding her to his chest.

"I don't care. This is my restaurant, and I'm responsible for whatever happens here. I won't let anyone get hurt in my restaurant. Let me go." Nes's eyes were black with fury as she struggled to get out of Gawen's hold on her.

"But I—" His voice choked off on a pained groan, and Nes tore out of his arms and hurried toward the corridor. Gawen put a hand on the table and leaned against it for support while he cupped his groin with his other hand, making it obvious what Nes had done to get away from him.

"Fuck." Henry let go of her hand and stormed after his sister, but before either of them could reach the corridor, Duncan emerged with Julianne cradled in his arms.

Julianne was resting her head against Duncan's

shoulder, but her eyes were open, and she looked all right, unless you counted the shocked expression on her face.

"What happened?" Sabrina walked up to the couple while studying Julianne's face. "What did she do to you? Are you hurt?"

Julianne shook her head when she met Sabrina's gaze. "I don't think so. She was suddenly in front of me, and then she was in my mind. But she couldn't do it. When she let me go, she hissed something about true mates being an abomination before she escaped through the back door. So, I'm fine." She looked up at Duncan and smiled. "We're fine."

Most of the people in the room seemed to breathe a sigh of relief. Except Jennie, who was staring at the entrance to the corridor with concern lining her face. Trevor hadn't come back yet and neither had Leith or Aidan. Which probably meant that they had gone after Amber to try to catch her.

"That's fantastic." Sabrina nodded, but her expression was tight with worry. "I have to find Leith." She hadn't taken more than two steps, though, before Leith and Trevor came back into the room.

"Thank God." The blond witch threw her arms around Leith's neck, and he wrapped his arms around her and leaned his cheek against her head.

Jennie let out a muffled scream before she ran to Trevor and threw herself into his waiting arms.

Eleanor moved over to Henry where he was standing next to Leith and Sabrina. "What happened to Aidan?"

Leith met her gaze. "He is following Amber at a distance. Three people running down the street after a woman would attract too much attention, and we cannot confront her in the middle of Wick anyway. He will contact us as soon as she stops, he loses her, or he can tell where she is heading. We should get ready to leave."

Henry put his hand on the small of Eleanor's back and guided her back to where she had been sitting. "Put this on." He handed her the blanket that had been hanging on the back of her chair.

She frowned as she looked into his eyes. His expression was unreadable, but there was a tick in his jaw that sent an icy tendril of fear up her spine to settle at the base of her neck.

Without arguing, she pulled the blanket over her head until she was fully covered. She wanted to ask Henry what was wrong, but it was better to wait until they were back in the car. At least then she would have his full attention.

Henry led her out the door and down the street. Eleanor could hear cars passing and people talking like this was just an ordinary summer day in this little lazy town. They had no idea there was a serial killer on the loose among them, but then they weren't the target of Amber's wrath and need for revenge.

A car door opened, and Henry helped her into the seat before closing the door behind her. Eleanor waited until he had entered the car on the other side and closed the door before she removed the blanket.

Henry still had the same unreadable expression on his face, and he didn't meet her gaze when she put her hand on his.

Eleanor didn't think Sabrina and Leith had entered the car yet, but even if they had, she still needed to know what was going on with Henry. His cold demeanor was scaring her and reminding her too much of how he had acted earlier that day. Was he having second thoughts about spending time with her again? Or had he realized that she didn't mean anything to him other than someone he was physically attracted to.

"Henry, what's wrong?" She couldn't help the slight tremble in her voice.

His brows drew together, and he lowered his gaze to her hand on top of his. "I… I think it might be best if we don't spend any more time together than is strictly necessary."

His words had the same effect as a fist to the stomach, making her hunch over against the pain and nausea. "Why?" She forced the word through her tight lips.

"The only bond strong enough to withstand Amber's attack is the true mate bond. She has just proven that."

"I know." Something inside her shattered as she realized what he was saying, and she pulled her hand away from his. He didn't want to be tied to someone who wasn't his true mate. The fling they had agreed on and she had secretly hoped would grow into something more was already over before it could truly start. And he didn't have to spell it out for her to understand that she needed to find a way to break the vampire bond as soon as possible.

Unshed tears were clogging her throat and she had to swallow several times before she could speak. "Can I borrow your phone?"

CHAPTER 32

Henry

Henry squeezed his eyes shut for a second before pulling his phone out of his pocket and handing it to Eleanor.

It was for the best if Eleanor found a way to break the vampire bond so she could leave and not end up being Amber's target again. It was just sheer luck that the beautiful vampire hadn't already turned to ash as a result of Amber's actions.

And now that the evil bitch had found out she couldn't break a true mate bond, she was likely to shift her focus to the people who didn't have that kind of bond to tie them together. Which meant he and Eleanor were prime targets, and he couldn't stand by and let anything happen to his vampire.

His. He had called her his. But she wasn't. And her short response when he told her they shouldn't spend time together proved that.

He didn't matter to her as much as she did to him. It was that simple, and he should have realized that already. But it hadn't prevented him from hoping she would protest and tell him she didn't care and wanted to spend time with him anyway. He wouldn't have been able to say yes, of course, not with the threat Amber represented to Eleanor's safety, but it would have been a comfort to know that she wanted him as well and wasn't ready to give him up so easily.

"It's Eleanor again. Have you been able to find a solution to my problem?"

Henry couldn't make out the reply. He could only hear a soft murmur from where he was sitting, and although he was eager to know what was being said, he wasn't going to lean in to try to catch the words.

"Well, I need some answers, and I can't leave until I have them." Eleanor's eyes narrowed.

She listened to the other person for a while before she huffed and shook her head. "It's the middle of the day, and I can't travel. But I'm not leaving until this bond is broken anyway. And no, for the hundredth time, I did not mean for this to happen."

Eleanor's fist tightened in her lap as she listened again.

"Then tell him there's an enforcer in the area. If he wants me to show up soon, he'll have to help me find a way to break this bond. Otherwise, he can leave me alone and get someone else to do his dirty work." She ended the call before closing her eyes and letting her head tip forward as her shoulders sagged.

Henry wanted to pull her into his arms and tell her everything was going to be okay, but that would be a lie. At least it didn't seem like the bond between them would be broken just yet, and he couldn't help the smile forming on his lips at that knowledge.

He took a deep breath and schooled his features before he spoke. "Does your sire want you to go to him?"

She nodded slowly but didn't turn to look at him. "Probably, but he's not the one who's giving me orders at the moment. I won't go, though, until the bond is broken, and he will most likely stay away as long as Aidan is close by."

Henry frowned. "What happened between Aidan and your maker? It sounds like your maker is scared of him."

Eleanor chuckled, but there was no amusement in the sound. "You could say that. Aidan and his fellow enforcers kicked my maker's butt almost three hundred years ago for being a sadistic bastard and gathering followers who were willing to do practically anything for him, including murder, rape, and torture. Unfortunately, my sire and a few of his most diligent followers escaped before the enforcers could kill them, and now my maker has regained enough strength to start gathering followers again."

Henry was rendered temporarily speechless. She had already mentioned that her maker had no trouble killing people, so her elaboration of his activities didn't come as a big surprise. But three hundred years ago? Did that mean she was more than three hundred years old? He had sort of concluded that she was older than him, but he hadn't expected it to be by centuries.

"Um…" It took him a few seconds to come up with the right question. "Can I ask how old you are?"

Laughing, she finally turned to look at him. "Three

hundred and twenty-nine years old. But it will sound better if you just skip the first digit. And it is sort of correct since I was twenty-nine when I was turned into a vampire."

Henry nodded slowly, unable to tear his gaze away from her laughing face. "That's…slightly older than me."

All signs of amusement drained from her face, and she looked away. "Well, there's no reason to worry about the age difference anymore, is there? It's not like we're dating or anything."

Her derisive tone made him frown. It almost sounded like she was angry with him for telling her they shouldn't spend much time together, when just a minute ago he had gotten the impression that it didn't really matter that much to her.

The doors to the front of the vehicle opened, and Henry inwardly swore at the interruption. He wanted to find out more about what Eleanor really felt about him, but he didn't want to question her about that while they had an audience.

"We will head out of Wick," Leith said when he got into the car. "There is a place we can park not far from the river that will allow us the privacy to talk while we wait for Aidan to contact us."

"Sounds good." Henry let his head tip back against the headrest and closed his eyes. If only he had met Eleanor at a different time. Even though she wasn't his true mate, he would have liked to be able to spend time with her and get to know her without being in the middle of an ongoing emergency.

The best thing for him to do was to search for his true mate to secure his future with someone who would truly accept him for who he was. But his eagerness to keep searching had steadily diminished since he met Eleanor. And if he was going to be completely honest with himself, he could no longer stomach the thought of being intimate with another woman.

But that was bound to change as soon as he met the one who was supposed to be his, wasn't it? Then he would be able to forget about Eleanor, and his attraction to her would die.

He winced as his stomach rolled at the thought of losing the beautiful vampire beside him. He didn't know when his feelings had changed from mere lust to something more. But they had. And his whole body was tense with how much he wanted to reach out and wrap his arms around her and never let go.

Silence reigned in the car for the twenty minutes it took to reach the place Leith had mentioned. Eleanor wouldn't be able to leave the car while it was still sunny, and he would stay with her and keep her company, and perhaps get a chance to ask her about her feelings.

He was dreading her answer, though. There were signs that her feelings for him ran deeper than a superficial attraction, but at the same time she had been adamant that whatever this was between them was temporary, and she would leave as soon as their bond was broken.

The whole thing was confusing, and he didn't know what to believe. He wanted to hang on to the illusion that she cared about him for a little longer, but in reality it might be better to rip the Band-Aid off sooner rather than later.

"You can safely open the door on your side, Henry." Leith's voice sounded from the front. "I have parked close to a tree in order to make sure your side of the vehicle is in the shade."

"Thank you, Leith." Eleanor smiled. "I really appreciate what you do to ensure my safety and comfort."

"You are most welcome."

Leith and Sabrina both got out of the car, and Henry was just drawing in a breath to ask the crucial question when there was a knock on his door.

Frowning in irritation at the interruption, he opened the door to see Fia standing outside smiling at him.

"Would you mind if we switched places? I would like to talk to Eleanor for a little while." Fia leaned to the side and looked past him into the car. "If you don't mind, Eleanor."

"Of course not," Eleanor answered before he could say anything. And his spine stiffened when he picked up the relief in her voice.

Giving Fia a sharp nod, Henry got out of the vehicle and hurried away. His body felt numb, and his mind was spinning with all the reasons Eleanor was happy to be rid of him. Because of course she was. He was just a kid compared to her. A stupid kid who treated her well one minute and badly the next. What would she ever want with him anyway? He had nothing to offer her.

His stomach cramped, and nausea rolled through him. And for every beat of his heart, pain ripped through him like his veins were filled with shards of glass cutting into his heart with every beat.

Henry steered clear of the other people gathering beneath a couple of trees and headed toward the riverbank. He needed time alone just to breathe through the pain and try to regain some semblance of control. And he couldn't do that with other people around. People who lived and breathed happiness and contentment. People who had a future, something he was starting to doubt he would ever have.

CHAPTER 33

Eleanor

Eleanor breathed a sigh of relief when Henry left the car and Fia took his place. She welcomed the distraction from Henry's rejection. She still didn't know how to break their bond, and she was trying to forget the fact that she had to drink from him again when he clearly didn't want her to.

"Did I interrupt something? I can go get Henry again if you two need to talk." There was concern in Fia's voice.

Forcing a smile, Eleanor turned to meet the other woman's gaze. "No, it's fine. It's just…complicated."

Fia chuckled. "It usually is. But don't let that stop you. Henry can't take his eyes off you. You've got his full attention, and I believe it runs a lot deeper than mere desire. Have you considered the possibility that you might be mates? There is something about your colors that suggests you're connected somehow."

Eleanor frowned. "What do you mean by colors? We don't really look the same, and why would that matter anyway?"

The red-haired witch laughed. "I'm sorry. I didn't mean to confuse you. One of my abilities as a witch is to sense people's intentions, or personality if you will, as colors. The lighter the color the more good intentions compared to bad and vice versa. I've never really paid attention to the specific color people have before, though, whether it's red or blue or any other color, but perhaps I should have. Because lately I've noticed that true mates have matching colors. One might be lighter than the other, but they're the same color."

Eleanor's frown deepened. "And I have the same color as Henry? There must be a lot of people with the same color, though. And it's not like I would have a special connection with all of them."

"True." Fia nodded. "But your colors match exactly, and combined with the obvious attraction between you two and the way you behave around each other, I wouldn't be surprised if you're true mates."

Warmth spread through Eleanor's chest, and she had to swallow hard to prevent tears from filling her eyes at how much she wanted that to be true. It would be a disaster, considering what her maker would try to do to Henry when he found out, but she couldn't help the spark of hope anyway.

"But…" Eleanor's throat clogged, and she had to clear it before she could start again. "But I'm a vampire."

Fia laughed. "So? I'm human and a witch. I don't think it matters what you are so much as who you are.

And from what I've witnessed, I think you and Henry fit together perfectly. But this is, of course, just my opinion based on my observations."

Eleanor nodded slowly, her mind spinning with the possibility that it wasn't just the vampire bond tying her and Henry together. In fact, the vampire bond might be a result of the true mate bond, only snapping into place because they already belonged together.

"But that's not why I came to talk to you, though." Fia put a hand on Eleanor's arm. "I'm trying to figure out how Amber is suddenly able to break a mating bond. And I'd like to ask you a few more questions about what happened when you first met her."

"Okay, sure." Eleanor took a deep breath to try to focus on Fia, but it was difficult when all she wanted was to talk to Henry about what Fia had said. Or did she? Wouldn't he have already felt it if she was his true mate?

Fia took a deep breath. "Did you notice whether Amber used her power right before or after she and Erwin drank your blood?"

Frowning, Eleanor shook her head. "I'm sorry. I didn't really pay that much attention to what they were doing. She had chained me up, and I was trying to find a way to free myself. To no avail as you know, but that was my main focus at the time."

"Fair enough." Fia nodded. "I still need to ask, though, just in case you remember something that can help me understand how this is possible."

Eleanor forced a small smile. "Of course. Go ahead."

Fia nodded again. "Did Amber say anything to indicate what she had already tried in order to break the bond, and what she intended to try next when your blood didn't work."

Eleanor shook her head slowly while trying to recall what Amber had said that day several months ago. The woman had been furious, shouting abuse at both her mate and Eleanor. But there was one thing Amber had repeated again and again. *I will find out how this bond works, and I will destroy it.*

"I'm not sure if it's going to help you much." Eleanor studied Fia's face. "But she kept repeating that she was going to find out how the bond works. And I'm guessing she finally managed to do that."

Fia's eyes widened in shock. "Of course. I should've made the connection earlier. You know the couples she has killed? Amber hasn't just been siphoning power from them as they mated. She has been studying the power released as the bond forms. And she actually found out how it works. But the true mate bond doesn't work the same. It's already in place before the act of mating, which means she hasn't found a way to break it. And thank God for that."

There was a knock on the door on Fia's side of the vehicle.

Fia opened the door to reveal Sabrina standing outside with her brows pushed together in concern. "Aidan lost her, so we're back to not knowing where Amber is. Callum and Vamika are doing their thing to try to locate her, but for now we're waiting and hoping the evil bitch doesn't turn up unannounced."

CHAPTER 34

Henry

Henry's chest hurt. It felt like something heavy had been placed on top of him and was preventing him from drawing air into his lungs. He could manage shallow breaths but nothing more.

"Fucking assholes. Thinking they can outsmart me. Well, they'll soon realize their mistake."

There was something familiar about that voice, but he couldn't remember where he had heard it before. Not when he was struggling to get enough oxygen. Had he been unconscious for a while? Or sleeping perhaps? He must have been because his mind was sluggish, and he couldn't fathom where he was. There was a damp smell that was unfamiliar and didn't bring back any memories. So, how had he ended up where he was?

"If only this deadweight would wake up. How am I going to make use of you when you're unconscious?"

Her voice was full of disgust. "Because I'm not going to heal you. Not when I'm going to kill you soon anyway."

It was a good thing he didn't have the energy to move, or he would have surely done something to alert the woman to the fact that he was conscious when he suddenly realized who she was.

Amber. The voice belonged to Amber. And she was probably the one responsible for his less-than-adequate ability to breathe. But how had she managed to take him? And had she hurt someone else in the process?

Eleanor.

Suddenly, everything came back to him, and his lungs ceased to function altogether. He had left her in the car with Fia and walked down to the river to be alone for a little while.

After walking along the riverbank for about two hundred yards, he had sat down to try to think rationally about what had happened with Eleanor and what to do next. He could recall sitting there for a while before deciding to go back to the others. But he couldn't remember actually getting up and walking back. Was that when Amber had shown up and taken him?

Henry's need for oxygen became acute, and he tried to pull air into his lungs but to no avail. It was like his lungs had completely collapsed, and there was no longer any room for air at all.

"No. You're not going to die on me. Not yet." A hand slapped his chest hard before settling against his breastbone. Then a tingling feeling spread through his chest, and just a few seconds later it was like his lungs inflated, and he was able to pull sweet air into his lungs again.

"There. Now wake up." She slapped the side of his face hard, causing his head to roll to the side.

Henry didn't know whether he was going to be able to open his eyes. His face felt stiff and numb. But even if he was able to, he wasn't going to yet. Amber obviously wanted him for something, and whatever it was would end up hurting or killing someone. He had to find a way to prevent that. But he wasn't sure how.

He could pretend to stay unconscious for a while longer, but in the end, she would just kill him if he didn't respond. And although that was better than helping Amber hurt someone else, there had to be a better option.

What was she likely to use him for? There was one obvious answer to that question. Blackmail. She would threaten to kill him to force the others to do something for her. But in order to blackmail them, she would have to show them that he was alive. Or at least it would provide a better reason for them to comply with her wishes.

But what did she want? Her ultimate goal was to kill shifters, and his friends were the main people who stood between her and that goal. Luring them into a trap and killing them would serve her purpose. But how could he prevent her from doing that?

His friends weren't stupid. When she made contact and threatened to kill him, they would realize it was a trap. But being as loyal as they were, they would still try to save him. And he couldn't let them do that. The best thing to do was to make sure they didn't show up to rescue him. And the best way to do that was to provoke Amber into killing him.

It took him two tries to pry his eyes open and get a look at where he was. And as soon as he did, he understood the damp smell. He was lying on the floor in what looked to be a root cellar or something similar. Although it wasn't of the really old variety with a dirt floor. This room had a concrete floor and stone walls. There were no windows that he could see.

Henry opened his mouth and forced out one word to get Amber's attention. "Bitch." He would have liked to put more force and feeling into that word, but unfortunately, he didn't have the energy, and his throat was too rough to manage more than a whisper.

Laughing, she walked over to him and looked down at where he was lying on the floor. "Ah, so you're finally awake. How are you feeling? Any pain at all?" Her tone was mocking, but it made him think.

His chest had been hurting earlier because he couldn't breathe. But apart from that he was remarkably pain free, which was a little worrisome, considering he had no energy and just the thought of lifting a finger felt like hard work.

He focused all his energy on his right hand and tried to move his fingers. But although he could tell where his hand was, he had no control over it. Concern took over his mind and caused his eyes to widen as he stared up at Amber. His head was still rolled to one side, making it hard to see her clearly.

She laughed again. "Yes, you should be worried. Your neck is broken. I know it will eventually heal because you're a shifter, but I won't let you live long enough for that to happen unless you speak to your friends on the phone and tell them to meet me. Do we have a deal?"

He didn't exactly have a lot of choice. But then again it was exactly what he had expected to happen. Except he hadn't realized how injured he already was. It didn't prevent him from carrying out his plan, though. He could talk and that was all he needed. "Yes, we have a deal."

"Good." She pulled out her phone. "Make sure you do exactly what I tell you, and you'll be back with your friends in no time." Her lips stretched into a nasty smile.

She had no intention of letting him heal or get back to his friends. But he could pretend he didn't know that for a little while longer. "Okay."

Amber raised the phone to her ear. It didn't take more than a couple of seconds before someone answered.

"Julianne. So nice to speak to you again. How are you?" Amber was objectively speaking a good-looking woman, but the vicious sneer on her face would have made him shudder if his body had functioned well enough to let him.

He couldn't hear what Julianne said, but from the way Amber's eyes narrowed, she was probably telling the witch exactly what she thought of Amber's attempt to break Julianne and Duncan's bond.

"Well, I'm sorry you think so." Amber chuckled. "But I'm afraid your opinion doesn't really matter to me. And anyway, that's not why I'm calling. Have you seen Henry lately?"

Keeping an eye on Amber's face, he couldn't help wondering how long he had been unconscious. Amber wasn't known for her patience, so if he was to guess, he'd say probably an hour. But he had no way of knowing, so it was impossible to know whether the others had even discovered he was gone yet.

"I'm happy to inform you that he's right here next to me. He's not in the best of shape, though. I think his neck might be broken. But I'm sure he'll heal in no time after you've done me a small favor. I'll let Henry tell you all about that. I'm sure you would like to hear his voice to confirm I'm telling you the truth."

Amber crouched by his side and put her phone to his ear. "Now tell them I want to meet Leith in half an hour right outside your sister's restaurant in Wick. He will meet me there alone or you will die."

Henry didn't react to Amber's demand since it was along the lines of what he had expected. "Did you hear that?"

"Henry, are you all right?" Duncan's voice sounded through the phone. Julianne had probably put the phone on speaker so everyone could listen in.

Henry stared blankly at Amber as he spoke into the phone. "Go to Glasgow and kill Mary immediately. And if you don't, I will as soon as I get out of here."

The shock on Amber's face only lasted a second before her face contorted with fury. "Don't you dare, you piece of shit. You die now."

This time when she slammed her hand against his chest, there was no gentle tingling feeling of healing, but a vicious burning sensation that radiated out from his chest to every part of his body.

Screams of agony tore from him, but they soon stopped when he didn't have any more air to power them. He had expected her attack to be brutal, but for some reason he hadn't expected the sheer magnitude of pain that raked through his body like his veins had been filled with molten lava.

Eleanor. Henry screamed her name in his mind since no sound would pass his lips.

"And that vampire mate of yours will die with you." Amber snarled the words in his face. "What's with you people and true mates? It's disgusting. I thought it was supposed to be rare."

His heart stuttered in his chest, and he didn't know whether it was because of the shock Amber had just given him or because of her magic burning his body to a crisp. *Mate. True mate. No, she can't be my mate. She's not supposed to die with me.*

When his heart gave out, a single tear fell from his eye before he was plunged into a sea of darkness.

∞∞∞∞

Eleanor

Eleanor gasped when pain slashed through her chest like someone had just cut her open with a sword. She was struggling for breath, even though she didn't need to breathe, and her heart felt like it was on fire.

"What's wrong? What's happening to you? Why are you bleeding?" Fia's voice was filled with fear. "I'll find Henry, and Steph might be able to—"

The door on Fia's side was yanked open. "Henry is…"

Eleanor didn't hear the end of Bryson's sentence, but she already knew what he came to say.

Henry was dead.

A strong convulsion pitched her body back against the seat before a burst of power shot from her chest and took her consciousness with it.

CHAPTER 35

Gawen

Gawen stared at Eleanor's face. Her features were relaxed like in sleep, but he couldn't tell whether she was sleeping, unconscious, or dead. Except as far as he knew a dead vampire would turn to dust almost immediately, so she must still be undead.

He didn't know what to do for her, though. She didn't have any visible wounds, even though blood had leaked from her eyes, nose, and ears. It had started when Henry died, but it had stopped soon after when she had lost consciousness.

Gawen let his head tip forward and closed his eyes against the sense of loss that had taken hold of him. He still had trouble accepting that Henry was dead, the alpha who had been quick to accept Gawen into his pack, even though he knew nothing about him.

But there was no reason to doubt what he had heard on the phone. Henry's horrible screams of anguish and Amber's promise to kill him. It had been all too clear what was happening, and there was no reason to expect Henry to have survived. The connection was lost right after Amber said Eleanor was Henry's true mate, which made Henry's death, if possible, even more tragic.

Opening his eyes again, Gawen lifted his head from his chest to study the vampire's peaceful features. Her expression seemed to be at odds with the fact that she had just lost her true mate. But being unconscious, she didn't know that yet. It would be a horrible shock, though, when she woke up.

Someone else had just been given a horrible shock as well. Henry's sister. Leith had wanted to be the one to tell Nes about her brother's death, since he was the only one who had met her before they all had lunch at her restaurant. Gawen had left to take care of Eleanor before Leith made the phone call, but he could imagine Nes's reaction to the news.

Gawen raked his fingers through his hair. As much as he wanted to be there for Eleanor, he felt an almost unbearable need to comfort Nes. It didn't matter that Henry's sister had a less-than-favorable opinion of him. The knowledge that she was in pain was tearing at him and pushing him to go to her.

But for once listening to his feelings wasn't the right thing to do. He had always felt a need to heal and comfort people. It had been a part of him for as long as he could remember, and he knew it was one of the reasons people called him weak. They viewed him as soft and too much a slave to his emotions.

What they didn't understand was that emotions ruled everything and everyone. A lot of people prided themselves on making rational decisions unaffected by emotions. But it was a lie. Very few people were that cold, and even though they didn't realize it, their feelings colored all their opinions and decisions.

Which was one of the reasons he wouldn't go to see Nes. She needed people around her she cared about and who cared about her while she was grieving, not someone she had just met and didn't like.

Eleanor's whole body jerked, and he snapped his head around to look at her. She blinked her eyes a few times before she turned her head to look at him. "We need to find Henry."

CHAPTER 36

Henry

Henry's eyes flew open, and he stared at the stone wall for several seconds before he remembered where he was and what had happened. He was shocked that he had woken up at all. Amber had tried to kill him, and he had been sure she would succeed. So why had she stopped before he was dead?

The room was completely quiet, and even though he couldn't turn his head to look around, he got the feeling he was alone. But unfortunately, that didn't help much when he couldn't move. And based on the lack of pain he was feeling, it would still take a while for him to heal enough to even lift a finger. He would be stuck there until he could make his own way out of the building. Unless Sabrina could locate him, but there was no reason for her to try when they all thought he was dead.

Tears sprang to his eyes, and his lips stretched into

a wide smile when he recalled what Amber had told him. Eleanor was his true mate. If he had been able to, he would have jumped to his feet and danced around like a crazy person. Without even realizing it, he had achieved his ultimate goal. No wonder he had been so infatuated with her. She was his. All he had to do was find her and tell her.

Henry frowned. Except she hadn't seemed too interested in being with him the last time they spoke. Which meant he would have to do everything in his power to prove himself to her and make sure she wanted to spend the rest of her life with him.

His frown deepened. There was another issue, though. She was immortal, but he wasn't, and he had no idea what that would mean for them as mates. Would she die when he died, or would he become immortal as well?

Henry blew out a breath. He sincerely hoped it was the latter, because he didn't want to be responsible for shortening her lifespan. That would be a cruel fate for both of them.

His eyes widened when footsteps could be heard from the level above the room he was in. His heart sank to the pit of his stomach. There was still someone in the building. And that someone was most likely Amber.

"Fuck!" Henry squeezed his eyes shut in irritation. Why couldn't he just get a break? All he wanted was to spend time with his true mate. But that evil bitch was still around, most likely to prevent him from escaping.

Why on earth hadn't she killed him when she had the chance? It just didn't make any sense. She wasn't known for sparing people, so why would she keep him alive after he threatened her daughter?

"Henry."

His eyes snapped open when Eleanor's voice called his name. Could it really be her? Or was this just a cruel trick of his imagination? Wishful thinking perhaps.

"Henry, where are you?"

He grinned when he realized he had been too busy wondering if his ears were deceiving him to answer her the first time.

"I'm here." The words were more like a whisper, and he sucked in a breath before he tried again. "I'm here."

Running could be heard from the floor above before a door was yanked open and someone thundered down the stairs toward him. The door to the room he was in flew open and smashed against the wall.

"Henry." Eleanor's face was suddenly right in front of his. "Oh, Henry."

His smile faded along with his hope when her face crumpled, and pink tears trailed down her cheeks. "What's wrong?" He had thought she would be happy to see him, but that didn't seem to be the case. And he could only assume it had something to do with how she felt about him.

"You're..." She shook her head and swallowed before trying again. "You're hurt."

"Yes." Henry lifted an eyebrow at her, wondering why she was stating the obvious. Amber had told them as much on the phone and that was before the witch had said she was going to kill him.

Letting her eyes wander down his body, Eleanor

swallowed again before bringing her gaze back to his with anger turning her eyes a glowing red. "I don't ever want to see you like this again."

Henry stared at her, not sure what she meant by that. Was she angry with him because he was hurt or was this her way of telling him that she never wanted to see him again? A sharp pain suddenly seared through his chest like his heart had caught fire, and he clamped his jaws shut to prevent himself from screaming.

"Open your mouth, Henry." Eleanor narrowed her gaze at him. "Now!"

There was power in her words, encouraging him to do what she wanted. But she wasn't trying to manipulate him using her vampire abilities, and he could have resisted if he wanted to.

She bit into her wrist while staring into his eyes. When she lowered her wrist toward him, blood was covering her lips. "Open!"

He did as she demanded while keeping his eyes on hers.

Pressing her wrist against his mouth, she nodded. "Now drink."

Her blood flowed into his mouth, and he automatically swallowed. He didn't know what he had expected her blood to taste like, but shock reverberated through him when her flavor exploded on his tongue.

Henry had never tasted anything so delicious. And only the juices from her pussy had ever had a similar effect on him. Every part of his body tingled, and he could practically feel how it healed him from the inside out.

But healing wasn't the only feeling overloading his brain. Pleasure licked through his veins and had his cock hard in seconds, throbbing with a need so strong he tried to move his hand to touch himself. But his hand wouldn't move. The function of his arms was apparently lagging behind the function of his dick.

Eleanor lifted her head to look at something on the other side of him, or as it turned out, someone. "Leave. We need to be alone."

Henry hadn't heard anyone else come down the stairs and into the room, but then he hadn't exactly been at the top of his game. And Eleanor had grabbed all his attention from the second she arrived.

"Okay." Bryson's voice was filled with concern. "But tell us if you need help with anything."

Eleanor's gaze returned to Henry's. "He'll be fine in a couple of minutes. You don't have to worry anymore. He's safe now."

Henry searched her eyes to try to find out what she meant by that. Did she really care about him, or was this just a rescue mission to her? He really hoped it was the former, because if it was the latter, he had a lot of work in front of him to convince her to become his.

Her gaze didn't leave his again until she carefully removed her wrist from his mouth. "Are you feeling better?"

After swallowing down the last of her blood in his mouth, he nodded. "Yes, much better." He lifted his hand and after taking a look at it to confirm that it looked the same as usual, he put it on his chest where Amber had put her hand and pushed her magic into him.

He could feel the burned edges of his shirt, but his

skin was whole without any noticeable scar tissue. There was no blood coating his skin, which surprised him. He would have expected there to be considering the excruciating pain he had been in.

"I'm pissed off with you." Eleanor's eyes were glowing with fury, and he jerked with apprehension when she placed her hand on his chest next to his. He was confident she wouldn't hurt him, but his less-than-pleasant experience with Amber was still too recent to be ignored.

Eleanor's eyes softened a little, but her gaze was still stern when she continued. "Bryson told me you deliberately provoked Amber into killing you. And…" She paused and licked her lips, drawing his attention to her luscious mouth. "You didn't tell me I'm your true mate."

"I…" He couldn't take his eyes off her mouth, hoping that she would close the distance between them and kiss him. He would have sat up and pulled her close if not for the fact that she was holding him down. She had never really shown him her true strength before, but she did now, and he knew without a doubt that he wouldn't be able to rise until she allowed it.

"Didn't you know, or did you intentionally conceal it from me?" She moved a little closer and his gaze rose to hers.

"I didn't know until Amber announced it after I made sure she would kill me." Eleanor flinched, but he didn't let that stop him. "I don't understand why she didn't kill me, though. She should've after I threatened her daughter. She was going to lure you into a trap, and I couldn't allow her to use me to do that. But if I'd known you were my true mate, I would've chosen differently."

Eleanor turned her head away and swallowed hard, before she looked back at him. "You're tied to me and thereby immortal. I neglected to tell you that because I was going to find a way to break the bond. Amber killed you, Henry, but you only stayed dead for a few seconds. Thankfully, those seconds were enough for her to leave and think you were gone. But I never want to experience your death again."

CHAPTER 37

Henry

His jaw dropped, and he stared at her completely dumbfounded. Immortal. *Holy shit.* So that was why he wasn't dead. It was hard to believe, though, and he probably would have needed more convincing if he hadn't experienced what Amber had done to him.

Eleanor's lips curled into a smile, and her tongue shot out to wet her top lip, drawing his attention back to how much he wanted to pull her close and fill his senses with her. His cock throbbed, ready for action, but he wasn't yet sure she wanted him.

"Eleanor. I—"

She palmed his erection, and whatever he had planned to say vanished in the wave of desire that raced through his body.

"Save your breath." She grinned down at him. "You will need it to feed your lungs while I punish you for what you have put me through the last few days."

"What?" His mind was reeling, trying to break through the fog of lust to understand what she was saying.

But before he had time to assess her intentions, she was straddling his legs and had his naked cock in her hand. He didn't even have time to be shocked at her speed before her thumb pressed against the base of his cockhead, and his whole body jerked with the resulting lick of pleasure.

"I'll tease you until you're about to go insane with your need for release." She winked at him. "And perhaps then I'll consider letting you come."

He groaned as her hand closed around the head of his cock before stilling. Her hand on him was enough to elevate his breathing, but he needed more. He lifted his hips to try to encourage her to caress his aching hard length, but instead she let go of him and yanked his pants down to midthigh.

He shuddered when her soft hand closed around his balls and started massaging them gently. It felt amazing, and he widened his legs as much as he could to give her space to fondle him. Go insane? That wouldn't take long.

When she leaned forward and gripped the base of his cock, he prayed that she was finished teasing him and had decided to take pity on him.

But he should have known better. Using only her tongue, she flicked his frenulum, making his cock jump with every soft impact. Then she licked slowly around the rim of his cockhead before returning to her gentle teasing of flicking her tongue against his increasingly sensitive flesh.

"Eleanor, please." His voice was rough and whiny

at the same time, which was an odd combination. "I just died. Please have some mercy on me."

She raised her head and narrowed her gaze at him. "And where was your mercy when you decided to die on me?" One hand kept fondling his balls while the other was still wrapped around the base of his shaft. "You can't expect there to be no consequences."

Eleanor lowered her head slowly while staring into his eyes. Then her tongue shot out and flicked hard at the base of his cockhead, and he gasped as a spike of pleasure raced through his body and sent him right to the cusp of release.

Holding his breath, he waited for Eleanor to repeat what she had just done to push him over edge, but nothing happened.

"Please." He choked out the word as need pounded through him and made the sound of his pulse loud in his ears. "Please let me come." If he didn't think she would thwart his attempt, he would have wrapped his hand around his hard length and given it the couple of tugs required to send him flying. Her teasing was fantastic, but he was getting desperate.

Eleanor chuckled. "I think you can handle a little more, don't you?" Her eyes narrowed again. "And don't you even think about touching yourself. That will just make me draw this out even longer."

Henry took a shaky breath and wet his lips. "What about you? Don't you think I'll return the favor when I get the chance? Two can play at this game you know."

She threw her head back and laughed, her curls bouncing around her head. "I should hope so, and I can't wait for us to have time to really play." Her eyes were filled with heat when they landed on his. "But if we start now, it will be hours before I let you out of here, and I've got a feeling your friends would get impatient."

He grinned at her enthusiasm, but his expression froze, and his body bowed off the floor when she suddenly leaned forward and sucked the head of his cock into her hot wet mouth. Her tongue danced around the rim, and his balls pulled up so tight that any farther and they would have lodged in his throat.

Gasping for breath, he tried to find something to hold onto, but the floor was bare, and he didn't dare grab ahold of Eleanor's head for fear that he would use his grip on her to force his shaft so hard down her throat that he would hurt her.

Her mouth had him on the brink of release in no time, and he rocked his hips in desperation while expecting her to pull away at any moment to continue her teasing. But she surprised him again when she took as much of him as she could into her mouth and sent him spinning into a sea of ecstasy that threatened to devour him.

His throat was raw from screaming his pleasure by the time he came down. And all the energy that had filled him when he drank Eleanor's blood seemed to have been pumped out with his seed, leaving him a drained hunk of flesh on the floor with lungs working like forge bellows.

A hand cupped his cheek, and he opened his eyes to smile up at Eleanor. She was grinning down at him with her eyes still glowing red.

"Are you sure I can't do anything for you?" He lifted his hand and pushed a lock of hair from her beautiful face. "I'd like nothing more than to make my true mate scream with pleasure."

Without saying anything, she slowly closed the distance between them before pressing her lips softly against his.

Curving his hand around her neck to make sure she didn't pull away, he moved his lips against hers. Kissing Eleanor suddenly had a different and more significant meaning. They hadn't mated yet, but knowing she was his was making his heart expand with a joy so great it was bringing tears to his eyes. The sheer magnitude of his fortune in finding her was threatening to blow his mind.

All too soon she broke the kiss and pulled her head back to look at him. "The others are worried about you. I told them you would be fine as soon as I gave you my blood, but I don't think they really believed me."

Henry sighed. "I guess it's time to get moving then." Pushing up on his arms, he took in the room he was in for the first time. "This isn't exactly the appropriate venue for our mating anyway. I want us to be somewhere more luxurious for that event."

He froze before looking at Eleanor with fear turning his blood to ice. "I'm sorry, I'm… Do you want to mate me? I should've asked before, but I…"

CHAPTER 38

Eleanor

Eleanor watched the blood drain from Henry's face as he struggled with his words before they died on his lips. She was no longer in any doubt that he cared about her. He had already shown her he did in a thousand small ways. She had just been too preoccupied with his safety and the effect of the vampire bond to believe it. And he had been afraid of tying himself to someone other than his true mate after experiencing the result of a mating that wasn't based on love and respect.

Staring into his hazel eyes, she reached up with one hand and buried her fingers in his soft red hair. "I'd love to be your mate, Henry. There's nothing I want more."

His smile was so bright she could have been looking at the sun, and his eyes radiated love and happiness when he wrapped his arms around her and pulled her into a tight hug. "I love you, beautiful. You have been occupying my mind and all my senses since the first time your delicious scent filled my nose. And now I'll never have to let you go. You've just made me the happiest man on earth."

There was still the nagging fear that her maker would come after Henry as soon as he found out about her love for the wolf, but she pushed that feeling away to be dealt with later. "I think you have a few friends who will claim they rightfully own that title, but as long as you're happy, I'm happy."

Henry chuckled and got to his feet, grabbing her hand to pull her up with him. "Good. Then let's go so I can introduce everyone to my true mate."

Eleanor nodded and let him lead her out the door and up the stairs to the hallway where Bryson, Fia, Leith, and Sabrina were waiting impatiently.

Bryson chuckled and shook his head when he saw them, and Fia's face lit up in a smile. Leith and Sabrina both breathed out a sigh in what Eleanor took to be relief.

"So, you decided it was your turn to scare the cattle this time?" Bryson smirked at Henry. "If I didn't know better, I would've thought Eleanor was torturing you. But apart from your ruined shirt, you look remarkably well for a dead man."

Henry's head snapped around, and his eyes were wide when they met Eleanor's. "Am I—"

"No." Eleanor couldn't help laughing at Henry's stunned expression. "You're not a vampire. Just an immortal shifter."

"Okay." Henry chuckled. "It didn't even cross my mind that I might have changed after dying and drinking your blood until Bryson's comment. Between movies and books, there are various methods for turning someone into a vampire, so I'm not going to pretend I know how it's done."

Eleanor smiled. "I think most of them have got it right. A vampire drinks a person's blood until they're on the brink of death, and then the vampire feeds the person their immortal blood. The transformation usually takes a day or two before—voila—the person has turned into an immortal leech with a fatal sun allergy."

Laughter filled the hallway while Fia shook her head slowly. "When you put it like that it doesn't sound nearly as sexy as it's made out to be in most books and movies. I hope you're not planning on doing any recruiting for vampirism, because I'm not sure it would be a good fit for you."

A new wave of laughter spread before Henry put his arm around Eleanor's shoulders and pulled her close. "There will be no recruiting. The only blood you will be drinking from now on will be mine."

Eleanor smiled up at him. "Sounds good to me. It's a good thing you're a shifter. Otherwise you couldn't be my only food source."

"Good." His eyes darkened as his brows pushed together. "Because I don't think I would be able to handle you drinking from anyone else. I'd rather be anemic than allow that to happen."

"Thankfully, that won't be a problem." Eleanor chuckled. "Because I wouldn't be able to watch you suffer. Which reminds me, we have a witch to kill. I can't wait to get my revenge on that sinister bitch."

"Get in line." Bryson's eyes turned almost black

with rage. "I think we all have our personal reasons to kill her by now. If only we could trap her in one place long enough to destroy her, but she always seems to find a way to escape."

"That is true." Leith nodded, his expression tight with anger. "I think we need to discuss with Aidan and come up with a sound plan. This cat and mouse bullshit has been going on for long enough. It has to stop."

Henry nodded. "I suggest we go back to my sister's restaurant and discuss it there. There's enough room for all of us, and I'm sure Nes can come up with a good enough excuse to persuade any other diners to leave without getting too upset. I'll compensate her for her trouble. And since I've already drawn Amber's attention to the place by suggesting we eat there, returning to the restaurant won't put my sister in any more danger than she already is. I'd actually feel better if I could keep an eye on her right now until Amber is taken care of."

Bryson grinned. "And if she has any more of that delicious food to offer, I'd be happy to have dinner there. I'm a multitasker with the ability to both eat and discuss the plan at the same time."

Fia burst out laughing. "Absolutely. You can even chew gum while riding in an elevator. It's impressive."

Raising an eyebrow, Bryson turned his head slowly to look down at his mate. "I'm glad you think so. Do you want me to elaborate on a few other multitasking skills I have? You never know, Leith and Henry might need some pointers."

Eleanor bit her bottom lip, and her pussy clenched when her thoughts diverted to what Henry had done to her in the bathroom at Leith's house and again in the car. He had yet to fill her with his cock, but she had a feeling she would have a fantastic time when he did. Henry was nothing if not attentive to her needs, so any pointers Bryson could give would be wasted on him. Her mate already knew how to drive her insane with need and give her the most mind-blowing orgasms.

The corner of Leith's mouth rose in a small smile. "Well, we can stand around here listening to Bryson elaborating on his skills in bed to his mate's embarrassment, or we can go to Nes's restaurant and enjoy her hospitality and delicious food. I prefer the latter option."

"Me too." Henry smirked at Bryson. "Whatever I lack in bicep strength compared to you I make up tenfold in agility. Now let's go get some food. Dying is exhausting and has left me starving. I don't recommend it."

Bryson grumbled something unintelligible when Henry tightened his hold on Eleanor and led her past the other couples toward the front door, where the blanket lay discarded on the floor.

Eleanor would have liked nothing better than to be able to head directly to a hotel and barricade them inside a room for a few days, but they had work to do. The shock of everything that had happened in the last few hours was still lodged as a tight ball of terror in her belly, and she feared it wouldn't dissolve until Amber was gone.

CHAPTER 39

Gawen

Gawen stayed at the back of the group when they entered Nes's restaurant for the second time that day. Her disdain when she had heard how he asked Fia to be his mate was still fresh in his mind, and he couldn't imagine her opinion of him had changed in the few hours since their last visit.

Nes already had her arms around Henry's neck when Gawen passed through the door. Tears were coursing down the woman's cheeks, and even though they were probably happy tears, Gawen's chest still grew tight with how much he wanted to comfort her.

He knew Leith had contacted Nes as soon as they found Henry and realized he was alive, but seeing her brother walking and breathing was different than being told he was okay. Gawen could imagine the anguish she must have felt during the time she thought Henry was dead.

After reluctantly releasing her tight hold on her brother, Nes threw her arms around Eleanor. "Thank you, Eleanor. Thank you for saving my brother. He's the only family I've got. Or at least the only one who matters. Leith didn't give me a lot of details on the phone, so you'll have to fill me in on the specifics of what happened."

"I will."

Gawen couldn't see Eleanor's face, but there was a smile in her voice.

"Right." Nes let her arms drop and took a step back. "Why don't you take a seat while I go get you some menus." She swiped at her tears while moving over to the counter.

Gawen pushed down his need to go to her and pull her into his arms. She didn't want his attention, and even if she had needed a shoulder to cry on, she wouldn't have chosen his.

By the time he walked over to the table, he noticed that everyone had chosen the same places they had occupied earlier in the day. Which meant he was sitting next to Nes again, unless she chose not to eat with them this time.

He sat down and waited silently for Nes to reach him and hand him a menu. Just the thought of her taking a seat beside him was enough for his cock to harden, and he squeezed his eyes closed and tried to will it to calm down.

A hand touched his shoulder, and he swirled his head around to look up into Nes's dark-blue eyes. They were still shiny with tears, and the sight made his heart clench. "I'm sorry for the pain you've suffered today."

She tilted her head a little to the side while holding his gaze. "Thank you, Gawen. And I'm sorry for hurting you."

It took him a second to understand what she meant. "Oh. There's no need to apologize. It was my own fault."

Frowning down at him, she shook her head. "No, it wasn't. You were trying to protect me. A little forcefully perhaps but you didn't deserve to be kneed in the balls for it. So, please accept my apology. I appreciate what you were trying to do."

A happy smile spread across his face. "Apology accepted."

Nes returned his smile as she handed him a menu before moving on to Julianne, who was seated next to him.

Gawen's stomach was filled with a warm fluttery feeling, and he couldn't stop smiling. Henry's sister wasn't angry with him like he had expected, and he suddenly realized just how worried he had been about seeing her again and possibly being subjected to her disapproval or anger.

Looking down at the menu, he tried to stop grinning like a fool. It was impossible, though. Harboring feelings for his alpha's sister was foolish, but he couldn't control how he felt. She seemed to draw his attention like the moon drew your eye in the dead of night.

CHAPTER 40

Henry

Henry stared down at his plate, which still contained half of his meal. He had been starving when they left the cellar where Amber had taken him, but after just a few bites, he'd lost his appetite, and it had nothing to do with the exquisite food.

It was hard to concentrate on anything other than Eleanor. He wanted to be alone with his mate and just enjoy the fact that he'd found the woman he was going to spend the rest of his life with. And he wanted to mate her and make her his for eternity.

Eternity. The word suddenly had a different meaning after finding out he was immortal. Shifters had a longer lifespan than humans, so he had already been fortunate in that respect, but being immortal was a whole different ballgame that he hadn't really been able to wrap his head around yet.

Pure happiness surged through him again, making

his heart rate speed up. It happened every few minutes when the thought of how lucky he was hit him.

Not only had he found his mate, but it had turned out to be Eleanor, the most beautiful and amazing woman he had ever met, and the only one he had ever considered giving up his search for his true mate for. That fact alone should have made him realize who she was to him. But with her being a vampire and the uncertainty regarding the effects of the vampire bond, it hadn't seemed plausible.

A hand smoothed over his thigh to settle between his legs, and he shuddered as hot desire surged through him. He was already hard and aching for her, and having her hand teasing him didn't make him want her any less.

Leaning toward her, he discreetly cleared his throat before speaking in a low voice. "Are you trying to embarrass me, beautiful?"

Eleanor chuckled before turning her head and looking at him with a red glow in her eyes. Her voice was little more than a whisper when she spoke. "I just can't seem to keep my hands off you. This is torture, and I'm not sure how long I'll last before I rip your clothes off and have my way with you in front of everyone."

A jolt of need had his cock swell even more in the tight confines of his pants, and he just managed to stop himself from groaning as an image of Eleanor riding him took over his mind. They needed time alone soon or he was going to burst the seams of his pants. Torture indeed.

He gripped her hand that had him close to spilling and pulled it away from his crotch. As much as he enjoyed her hand on his shaft, he couldn't take any more before they had the opportunity to rip each other's clothes off and fuck like bunnies.

Henry was just sifting through viable excuses for them to leave the room for a while when Aidan rose and cleared his throat for attention. *Oh, for fuck's sake. I just want to make love to my beautiful mate.* But he bit back his grumpy response and sat up straighter in his chair in an attempt to pay attention.

"As you all know by now, I lost Amber when she fled after trying to break Julianne and Duncan's bond." Aidan's gaze swung around the table until it came to a stop on Henry. "And the next thing she did was to seek out Henry in order to set a trap for Leith. I'm exceedingly grateful you're still with us, Henry, and that you've finally realized you and the pretty vampire by your side are mates."

Henry frowned. "You make it sound like you knew Eleanor was my true mate before I did."

The enforcer chuckled. "I can't claim that I knew without a doubt, but I think, like most of the other people around this table, I had a strong suspicion."

Several of the others smiled and nodded their agreement, and Henry felt his eyes widen in shock. Bryson had asked him whether Eleanor was his mate, but Henry hadn't realized the rest of them had been thinking the same thing. Although he probably should have.

"I'm happy you've reached the goal you set for yourself when we were nothing more than kids."

Nes's voice from beside him made Henry turn his head to smile at her. "I thought you were against mating?"

"I was and still am." She smiled. "But that doesn't mean I can't be happy for my brother when he gets what he's always wanted. Just don't expect me to follow in your footsteps, because I won't."

Henry chuckled. "What if you meet your true mate?"

She huffed and crossed her arms over her chest. "The chance of that is so low I'm not even going to consider it."

"You might want to." Letting his gaze swipe around the table, Henry took in all the happy couples. "Seems to me the probability of finding your true mate has drastically increased recently. Don't be too surprised if yours suddenly shows up in your restaurant one day, and you end up getting swept off your feet and into your happily ever after."

"I'm sorry to interrupt, but we have a witch to catch." Aidan lifted an eyebrow at Henry before he continued. "We need to find her and kill her as soon as possible, but in order to do that we need a plan that takes into account all her known abilities, her usual means of escape, and any known or likely weaknesses. There are a lot of powerful and resourceful people around this table, so destroying Amber without any of us getting seriously injured should be possible if we work together."

Henry nodded slowly. He agreed, but considering their track record against the evil bitch was less than impressive, it was easy to succumb to doubt. Amber had been able to injure or kill quite a few of the people around the table.

"We know where she's headed." Callum shared a smile with Vamika before looking at Aidan.

The enforcer's eyes widened in surprise. "Really? You seem very certain."

Callum chuckled. "It's obvious really. She's traveling south as we speak, and I'd be very surprised if she's not on her way to Glasgow to pick up her daughter. The fact that we're not like her and wouldn't kill an innocent woman unless we had no other choice eludes her for the simple reason that she's judging everyone else by her own standards. She doesn't care about innocent people anymore, if she ever did, so she thinks we are the same."

"That's an excellent point." Aidan looked impressed. "And very observant."

"Thank you." Callum smiled. "Unfortunately, Glasgow is a long way from Wick, and we don't know where Amber will be heading from there. She will pick up Mary and try to find someone to take care of her. It's unlikely Amber will choose a mental institution again, though, since she already knows it will make it easy for us to find her daughter. There are not that many such institutions to choose from in Scotland."

Duncan frowned. "We can't rule out that she'll go south of the border and continue her plans somewhere else, but if you ask me, I think she has realized that we won't give up and in order to really effectuate her plans, she'll have to neutralize us. She'll be back to get us as soon as she has found someone to take care of her daughter, and she knows how to use the element of surprise to get the upper hand. If we want to kill her, we need to turn the tables on her—let her think she is sneaking up on us when, in fact, we have set the whole thing up and are ready for her."

Steph leaned forward in her seat. "And we have to

prevent her from running, because that's usually how our encounters with her end. She lashes out and runs."

"Yes." Sabrina looked pensive. "And we have to take into account that she has the ability to locate each one of us. For all I know, she might be able to keep track of us continuously, but I doubt that's true for more than one or two of us at a time. We'll have to identify who she's most likely to keep an eye on, and I would think it's the people she considers to be the greatest threat to her and what she's trying to do."

"That description fits quite a number of people around this table, and Fia is one of them." Bryson crossed his arms over his chest with anger darkening his eyes. "Amber wouldn't have tried to persuade Fia to join her if she didn't consider my mate a worthy accomplice, or opponent as it currently stands."

"There is one argument counting against your theory though, Sabrina." Steph's brows pushed together. "If Amber could track someone that easily, she should've quickly realized that you were still alive after what happened at McFarquhar's Bed. Unless, of course, she was so sure of herself that she never bothered to check. I think she knows now, though. Otherwise, why would she ask for Leith to meet her in Wick? He should have been dead by now or at least severely incapacitated and no longer a threat to her."

Both Sabrina's and Leith's expressions tightened when they were reminded of what had happened at McFarquhar's Bed. And no wonder. Henry hadn't been there to witness Amber killing Sabrina, and he couldn't even begin to imagine what Leith had gone through watching it happen. One good thing had come out of it, though. Sabrina's death and subsequent immersion in water had triggered her transformation into a mermaid.

Henry turned to look at Aidan. "Does Amber know who you are and what you can do?"

The enforcer shook his head. "There were too many people around to risk doing anything to stop her earlier today. Eventually, she got into a car and sped off. She knows I'm with you, but I never got close enough to her for her to sense anything about me. And even if she had, she wouldn't have been able to tell what I can do, because I can guarantee you, she's never met anyone like me before."

"I think we need to pick a location for our showdown with her." Trevor had his arm around Jennie's shoulders, his concern for his mate evident in his tight expression. "And then we need some suitable bait to lure her in. Something that would make it impossible for her to resist without triggering her suspicion."

Eleanor wet her lips and tightened her grip on Henry's hand. "Amber wants power, and she wants to kill shifters. If she thinks she can have both at the same time without a significant risk to herself, that might be something that would get her attention. She'll know where we are, though, so unless we can find a way to block her ability to locate us, we'll have to make our presence nonthreatening and expected."

Henry smiled and studied Eleanor's profile. "I knew there was a reason I fell in love with you. Smart, beautiful, and a heart of gold. It's an unbeatable combination."

"That's three reasons." Eleanor's lips stretched into a smile when she turned her head to meet his gaze.

"And there are more." Henry's smile widened. "But we can go through those in more detail later."

CHAPTER 41

Eleanor

Eleanor's chest expanded as she stared into Henry's hazel eyes. They were filled with so much love that she felt tears prick the back of her eyes, and she swallowed to push them down before they decided to fill her eyes.

Somehow she had ended up having the love of a remarkable man, and it was still difficult for her to wrap her head around the fact that she was Henry's true mate. It seemed too good to be true, and in her experience that usually meant it was.

A hard rap on the door of the restaurant made her turn to look, but all she could see was the silhouette of a man outside against the lights behind him. At some point darkness had fallen without her noticing.

Nes started to get up. "I put a sign on the door that we are closed for a private function. But some people always need to have it spelled out to them."

"Let *me* go." Henry stood and put a hand on Nes's shoulder. "Just sit down and relax. I'll handle it."

Nes looked like she was going to argue, but then she smiled. "Thank you, brother."

Eleanor followed Henry with her eyes as he made his way over to the door. There shouldn't be any reason for her to worry now that Amber was on her way south, but unease still crept up Eleanor's spine and made the tiny hairs at the back of her neck stand up.

You're overreacting, Eleanor. Just relax. Repeating the mantra in her head, she watched as Henry unlocked the door and opened it.

"I'm sorry, but this restaurant is closed for a private function tonight." Henry's voice was calm and pleasant. "But you're welcome to come back another day."

"I'm not here for the food."

That voice. Eleanor was on her feet and already pushing Henry out of the way by the time the back of her chair hit the floor with a loud crack. "What are you doing here, David?" She stared at the familiar features of the man outside, her earlier unease suddenly making sense. She wasn't really surprised that someone had come for her after her phone call about the bond, but she hadn't expected it to happen so soon, and she hadn't expected it to be David.

"I've come to pick you up." David's features might as well have been set in stone.

When Eleanor had first met David, she had thought him remarkably good at hiding his emotions. But that was until she realized the truth. David didn't have any emotions to hide. He was as cold as a mannequin and had no will of his own.

And that was why he was her maker's favorite. David completed every task to the letter and never hesitated no matter how horrible his assignment was. The fact that David had come to pick her up was confirmation that her maker was fully aware of where she was, who she was with, and the vampire bond she had formed with Henry.

"That's not going to happen." Henry spoke from right behind her, and his voice was no longer pleasant.

David's gaze lifted from hers to Henry's. "You will come as well. This is not a request. I'm here to retrieve the both of you at any cost."

"Are you sure about that?" Aidan's voice surrounded her at the same time as his power filled the space around her and pressed against her chest, making her happy she didn't need to breathe.

David's eyes widened a fraction for a moment, but the change was so subtle she didn't think anyone who didn't know him would have noticed. "Yes. I have been ordered to bring these two to my master."

Aidan chuckled, but the sound was more sinister than joyful. "Then I'll have to repeat what Henry just told you. That's not going to happen. These two are under my protection. You can give your master a message, though. If he ever gets up to any of his old tricks, we will find him and kill him and anyone who willingly takes part in his revolting activities."

David gave a sharp nod. "I understand."

Pain bit into Eleanor's left forearm at the exact time she took a step back and pushed Henry away from her. She had expected David to lash out and had been prepared for his attack, but instead of severing her throat, his sharp claws had torn open the arm she had lifted to block him.

Before David could try again, she was flung out of the way, and Aidan had him by the neck on his belly on the floor. "The only reason you're still alive is that I want you to deliver the message to your master. Do you remember the message?"

"Yes." The word came out garbled, no doubt because David's face was mashed against the floor.

Aidan's hand tightened around David's neck, his fingers digging deeper into his flesh. "Will you deliver the message?"

There was a second of silence before David answered. "Yes."

Eleanor wasn't sure she believed him, though. Delivering a message like that would ruin David's standing with her maker, and his punishment would be severe.

"Do you need my blood to heal faster?" Henry moved in front of her, and she tipped her head back to meet his worried gaze.

"No, I'll be fine." She gave him a small smile and put her right hand on his chest. "You don't need to worry about me."

Aidan held on to David's neck while letting the man get to his feet. David's nose was broken, his lips were swollen, and there was a cut across one of his eyebrows, but the injuries were already healing.

"I don't trust you," Aidan sneered close to David's ear. And that was all the warning the vampire got before Aidan bit into his shoulder.

This time David's eyes noticeably widened in shock, but he quickly schooled his features back into the stony expression he usually carried.

Aidan pulled back and licked David's blood from his lips. "I'll be able to track you now. You won't be able to hide from me ever again. Do you understand what that means?"

The vampire tensed and visibly swallowed before he answered. "Yes."

"Good." Aidan turned David to face the door. "Then you realize that I'll know it if you ever approach these two again, and I'll take the appropriate action to stop you. I'll also know it whenever you kill someone, and when I come for your master, which believe me will happen eventually, I'll make sure you are punished for every death you are responsible for before I'll let you die."

Aidan paused, no doubt to let the significance of what he had just said sink in. "Now leave and deliver my message to your master. You have twenty-four hours. Your master will punish you, and I will know it when he does, and that's how I'll know you've delivered the message. If you're not punished, I'll find you and exact my own punishment before I kill you. You might be thinking that you're not left with a lot of choice, and you're right. However, you can choose to die right here right now. Would you like that?"

"No." David stared straight ahead, his body relaxed.

"Remember what you have agreed to. You know who I am." Aidan opened the door and walked David outside before letting go of his neck.

David stood completely still for a couple of seconds before he hurried down the street without looking back.

CHAPTER 42

Henry

As soon as Aidan came back inside and locked the door, Henry walked up to him. "Do you think he will be back for Eleanor?"

The lightning-quick attack on his mate had shaken him to his core, and his mind was still reeling with the fact that he would never be able to fight someone like that. His reflexes simply weren't quick enough. And although Eleanor had proven that hers were, it wasn't enough to remove the tension tightening all the muscles in his body.

Aidan tilted his head a little to the side, a frown pushing his brows together. "There's never any guarantee, but I believe David understands that my punishment will be worse than his master's for the simple reason that I don't need him alive and functioning afterward."

Henry nodded slowly, accepting Aidan's logic. It

wasn't enough to help him relax completely, but it helped.

A hand smoothed up his spine, and he turned to look down into Eleanor's warm brown eyes. "Don't worry about me, Henry. David is not much older than I am, so he doesn't have any real advantage over me except for the fact that he is cold as ice. And I believe Aidan is right, and David will stay away from us. My maker won't kill him because he's too useful, and David knows it. He's also fully aware of who Aidan is and what kind of damage he can do."

After taking a look at her forearm and seeing that the gashes were close to healed already, Henry pulled her into his arms and buried his face in the crook of her neck. He pulled her scent deep into his lungs and just held her close to try to ease the tension in his body.

The other people in the room were talking, but Henry didn't pay any attention to what they were saying as he focused on his breathing and the softness of his mate's body against his. His body slowly relaxed, but the proximity to his mate soon filled him with another type of tension. A more pleasant kind, but no less intense.

"Listen up, everyone." Nes's elevated voice caught Henry's attention, and he lifted his head to look at her. "As some of you have mentioned, you need a suitable place to stay the night, and I might have a solution. I'll have to check, though, so I can't promise anything yet, okay?"

Several people smiled and thanked his sister for trying to help them find a place to sleep.

Henry nodded. "Thank you, sis."

Nes smiled at him. "I'll be back in a few minutes." She hurried away before disappearing through the door to the kitchen.

Eleanor's fingertips brushed over his forehead, drawing his gaze back to hers. "You're sweating. Are you in pain?" There was a deep crease between her brows as she studied his face.

Frowning, he opened his mouth to tell her no, but the word got stuck in his throat when his belly twisted into a knot, and he winced at the pain.

"You are." Her eyes darkened, and she put a hand on his chest and pushed. "Let's go and sit down. As soon as I take a little of your blood, you'll feel better."

Henry let his arms fall to his sides, releasing her. "Not here." He knew what would happen as soon as her teeth penetrated his skin, and that wasn't something he wanted anyone else to witness. Not when he had a choice.

Narrowing her eyes at him, Eleanor crossed her arms over her chest. "Here is the only option we have at the moment, and I'm not willing to wait and watch you suffer until we can find somewhere more private."

Shaking his head at her, he crossed his arms over his chest, mirroring her stance. "And I'm not willing to let you drink from me among all these people. It's not happening, so forget it. Until we can find a place to be alone, I can manage."

Eleanor's lips pressed into a hard line, but she didn't say anything to counter his declaration.

They were still standing there scowling at each other when Nes returned with a smile on her face. "I've got some good news. My server's sister is renting out a large farmhouse, but the people who were going to rent it this week canceled at the last minute. It's a little to the south but not far. What do you think?"

"Sounds perfect." Trevor grinned and put his arm around his mate. "I'd say let's go."

Henry nodded at his sister, and so did most of the others in the room. "Are you going to stay with us?"

"Yes." Nes nodded. "I've got the code for the door and the responsibility for all of you behaving." She grinned. "I'll pull the car up front, and you can all follow me."

Everyone headed out of the restaurant to get their cars. Henry and Eleanor followed Leith and Sabrina to their vehicle before getting into the back seat. All the plastic was still in place, giving them privacy from any prying eyes.

As soon as Henry had closed the door behind them, Eleanor straddled his legs, but before she could lean in, he shook his head at her. "Not yet. We'll be at the farmhouse soon." The words had barely left his mouth when his stomach cramped, and he clamped his jaws shut against the pain that seemed to radiate from his belly all the way to the extremities of his body.

"Henry please." Eleanor's voice was filled with a mixture of frustration and anger, and her eyes narrowed into slits. "This is unnecessary."

He shook his head at her again and forced his words out through his teeth. "I'll be fine for a little while longer."

"It doesn't look that way." She cocked her head, and her expression changed into one of concern.

Henry pulled in a deep breath and consciously loosened his jaw. "But I will be. It's not far." He reached up and buried his fingers in her mass of curly hair, almost moaning when the silky strands caressed his hand.

Eleanor's gaze dipped to his mouth, and the tip of her tongue licked across her bottom lip, making it shiny with wetness. Lifting her gaze to his, she leaned in slowly with an eyebrow raised in question.

A small smile stole across his lips, and he nodded. He would have to be close to death before he said no to a kiss from his mate, and even then he didn't think he would deny her.

Eleanor's mouth was just as soft as he remembered, and her kiss helped him shift his focus to her instead of the pain that pulsed through his body. Heat spread through him as their tongues played and danced, and his cock hardened, eager to be buried inside his mate.

A sting on the side of his tongue startled him, and the metallic taste of his blood filled his mouth. It was immediately followed by a need so strong he gasped into Eleanor's mouth. He grabbed her ass and pulled her close before grinding his aching shaft against her hot core. Desire burned through his body and pushed the pain away.

Eleanor took his head in her hands and pushed her tongue deeper into his mouth, moaning as she explored his mouth with an eagerness bordering on desperation.

CHAPTER 43

Henry

Henry was just about ready to rip Eleanor's clothes off and ignore the fact that they were in the back seat of Leith's car when the car stopped, and the engine cut off.

"Are you two lovebirds already naked, or are you decent enough to leave the car?" There was a hint of amusement in Leith's voice.

It took every ounce of Henry's willpower to pull his mouth away from Eleanor's, and the deep red glow in her eyes when she slowly opened them to glare at him told him she wasn't happy about the interruption either.

"We're decent." Henry's voice was so rough the words came out almost unintelligible.

"Good." Leith chuckled, and the front doors opened. "You will be happy to know that we have already arrived at the farmhouse, and you will soon have a bedroom all to yourself."

Leith and Sabrina got out, and the doors closed.

Henry chuckled when Eleanor's lips stretched into something that was most likely supposed to be a smile but looked more like a fierce warning with her fangs fully extended. "Beautiful, if I didn't know you're not about to hurt me, I'd be scared right now. You look like you want to devour me. A certain fairy tale comes to mind, except the roles are mixed up. I'm the wolf, and if anyone is going to eat Little Red Riding Hood, it's supposed to be me."

Eleanor burst out laughing. "What exactly are you saying? Are you comparing me to a wolf or Little Red Riding Hood?" Her eyes narrowed. "Or a grandmother?"

Henry's eyes widened. "I wouldn't. I would never—"

Eleanor's face split in a huge grin. "You're so cute when you're flustered." She climbed off his lap and opened the door. "Let's go. I want to find that room Leith was bragging about and strip you naked. It's about time I get to have you to myself for longer than a few minutes."

Henry's pulse increased, and his dick twitched. He quickly followed Eleanor out of the car and hurried after her toward the house.

Most of their friends were already inside. Only Gawen was still on the porch, looking like he couldn't decide whether he was welcome to enter or not.

"What's wrong, Gawen?" Henry looked at the man's face, but Gawen wouldn't meet his gaze.

"I…" The blond man frowned. "Your sister said there are only seven bedrooms. Even if someone stays on the couch, there still won't be room for all of us. I thought I might stay out here. Then I can keep an eye out while everyone's asleep."

Henry smiled and opened his mouth to respond, but Eleanor beat him to it. "Let's all go inside. I'm sure there are rooms that can be used for sleeping even if they're not bedrooms."

Gawen nodded at Eleanor slowly, but he didn't look convinced. "I don't want to make things difficult for...Nes." After glancing at Henry, the man looked down at his feet.

Even with his body so consumed by lust that he was barely aware of anything else, Henry didn't miss the smidgen of heat in Gawen's eyes when he mentioned Henry's sister's name.

Nes would probably resist any kind of attention from Gawen at first, but Henry wouldn't be surprised if it turned out that Gawen was exactly the kind of man Nes would fall for. Not that Henry could claim to know his sister's preference in men, but Gawen had a sincerity and gentleness about him that might encourage Nes to open her eyes to the possibility of mating.

"Come on." Henry put his hand on Gawen's shoulder. "I'm sure my sister is waiting for us. She likes to coordinate and direct people, so the longer we linger out here and delay her plan, the more irritated she will get. You don't want to upset Nes, do you?"

Gawen's eyes snapped to Henry's, and he shook his head. "No, of course not."

"Good." Henry smiled and took Eleanor's hand in his. "Then let's go." It might be unfair to use Gawen's conscience against him, but the man shouldn't have to feel that he needed to give way for everyone else.

From what Gawen had told him not long after they'd met, it was obvious that the man hadn't had an easy life and had always been made to feel inferior. But as Henry's pack member, that was going to change. Whether Gawen would end up with Henry's sister or not wasn't up to Henry, but as Gawen's alpha, he would make sure the man always had a place to call home.

Henry led the way into the large farmhouse, following the voices from down the hall.

Nes looked mildly irritated when they entered the living room where everyone else was already gathered, but Henry just smiled and winked at her, making her roll her eyes and shake her head.

"Okay. Now that everyone is finally here, we can decide who sleeps where." Nes smiled.

Duncan chuckled. "As long as I get to share a bed with my mate and don't have to spend all night looking at Trevor's ugly ass, I don't mind which room we're in."

Jennie snorted. "Well, you clearly haven't seen Trevor's ass if you say that. He has the sexiest—"

"Fine, fine." Duncan held up a hand to stop her. "There's no need to be explicit."

The rest of the room erupted with laughter.

"Yes, because you never are." Trevor shook his head as his shoulders shook with laughter.

"Hey, concentrate." Nes's voice was stern, but there was a hint of amusement in her eyes. "Don't you guys want to fuck?"

The room was deathly quiet for a second before laughter filled the room again with a few people shouting their agreement to the amusement of the rest.

Henry hadn't missed Gawen's reaction to Nes's question, though. The man's body had jerked, and his jaw slackened as he stared at Nes with desire darkening his eyes. But it had only lasted a few seconds before he lowered his gaze to the floor, and his shoulders sagged like in hopelessness.

The man might be more taken with Nes than Henry had first thought, but there wasn't much Henry could do about it. His sister had to make her own decisions and any encouragement from Henry to look in Gawen's direction might have the opposite effect. She wasn't one to take advice or even gentle nudging well, so Henry knew better than to try.

"There are five bedrooms upstairs suitable for couples." Nes smiled and swung her gaze around the room. "I don't know most of you, so I'll make a random selection. But don't worry. There are a couple of bedrooms here on the ground floor as well."

"Leith, Trevor, Michael, Duncan, and Henry. You'll be staying upstairs with your mates." Nes waved her hand toward the door of the living room. "Go on. We don't have all night. The rest of you stay here, and I'll show you where your rooms are."

Henry didn't linger, but immediately headed out of the room with Eleanor half running to keep up with his long strides.

They hurried up the stairs and entered the first bedroom they could find. It contained a large bed, which was all they required, but Henry wouldn't have cared if the room had been devoid of any furniture at all. The only thing they really needed was privacy, and they would finally have that.

As soon as he had closed the door behind them, he turned to Eleanor. She was staring back at him with hunger stark in her eyes, and it suddenly struck him that he was about to be mated. And to his true mate no less. All his dreams were coming true, and it was so overwhelming he had to swallow down his emotions to prevent tears from filling his eyes.

CHAPTER 44

Eleanor

"Henry." Eleanor closed the distance between them and put her hand on his cheek. "I still can't believe I'm going to have you with me forever. I never thought I would get the opportunity to be with someone, let alone someone as amazing as you. You're so much more than I ever even dared to dream of."

Henry blinked a few times and cleared his throat before he clasped her head in his hands and stared deep into her eyes. "You are my everything, and I think a part of me realized that as soon as I pulled in the first whiff of your scent. I just didn't understand what it meant. But how we got here doesn't matter anymore. We know who we are to each other now, and nothing is going to come between us again."

Putting her hands on his chest, Eleanor smiled up at him. "Does that mean I'll finally get to enjoy all of you? Because I must admit that I'm not sure I can wait any longer." And that was putting it mildly. She had wanted to rip his clothes off and fuck him since she had first met him, and their few stolen moments of enjoying each other hadn't been nearly enough. Not to speak of all the uncertainty and fear that had almost torn her apart.

Henry's hands landed on her hips, and his eyes heated. "You have my expressed permission to do whatever you want with me. That is"—he gave her a wicked grin—"as long as I get to eat you."

Eleanor's pussy clenched, and a shiver ran the length of her spine. "Deal." Her voice was so husky it was almost unrecognizable.

Before she could think what to do next, Henry lifted her and threw her toward the bed. Her back hit the mattress, but her bounce was cut short when Henry was suddenly on all fours above her, grinning down at her.

She blinked in surprise. Had he gotten faster? Or was her brain so affected by her need that she was starting to imagine things?

Her questions were soon forgotten when Henry covered her with his body and crushed his lips to hers. His demanding mouth devoured hers, and she squirmed as heat burned through her to settle between her legs.

Tearing her mouth away from his, she tried to wriggle out from beneath him. "Clothes… Too many clothes."

Henry chuckled, and the sound was decidedly wicked. "It sounds like you want to be fucked. Am I right?"

"Yes." Eleanor met his gaze, her hands already

tearing at his shirt. "I want you inside me, filling me to the brink."

He groaned, and his eyes turned almost black with need. "I can't wait to feel your pussy clamping down on my cock when you come."

Before she knew what was happening, he rose to his knees and pulled her up with him. After giving her a quick kiss, he lifted her shirt over her head and threw it onto the floor before cupping her breasts in his hands and thrumming his thumbs over her sensitive nipples.

She shivered as her nipples tightened into hard peaks and sent sparks of pleasure directly to her clit. Moaning, she pressed her thighs together against the insistent need centered between her legs.

Eleanor had never felt so desperate in her entire life. She didn't know whether it was a result of the vampire bond or the shifter mating bond, or perhaps a combination of the two, but whichever it was she couldn't wait any longer.

She grabbed Henry's shirt and ripped it clean off his body before reaching for the waistband of his jeans. But before she could rip that off, as well, Henry pushed her back. By the time she landed on her back on the bed, her pants and panties were halfway down her legs. Grinning at her, Henry backed off the bed and pulled her clothes off as he went, leaving her naked before him.

Eleanor narrowed her eyes at him. Henry had managed to undress her completely, whereas he still had his pants on. That had to be rectified. "Don't even think about coming back onto this bed before you have removed your jeans. I want to see the man I love naked."

He paused, staring at her. "You love me." It wasn't a question.

"You know I do." Smiling, she got up on her knees and made her way over to him, where he was standing by the end of the bed.

He nodded slowly, his throat moving as he swallowed hard. "I do, but you haven't said it before. I didn't know any words could sound that sweet."

"I love you, baby." She reached out and flicked open the button of his jeans before pulling the zipper down slowly until his cock sprang free. "I'll keep telling you that for the rest of your life, but right now I need you to make me yours."

Henry growled and quickly pushed his jeans down his legs before stepping out of them. "I'll make you mine, beautiful." He wrapped his hand around his thick length and gave it a couple of tugs. "And then I'll keep reminding you that you're mine until you beg me to stop."

His gaze lowered slowly down her body until it reached the black curls covering her most sensitive parts. "But first I need to taste you."

Eleanor sucked in a breath as her channel clenched and wetness pooled between her legs.

"Lie down and spread your legs for me, my beautiful mate." He grinned, showing teeth. "I'm hungry."

She did as she was told, lying back on the bed while keeping her eyes on his face. Henry was gentle and kind, but he had a predatory side that she enjoyed as well.

Homing in on her wet center, he pulled in a deep

breath. "Damn, your scent is almost enough to make me spill." He put one knee on the bed before lowering onto his elbows, putting his mouth only inches from where she wanted it. When he licked his lips, a shiver raced down her spine and she tilted her pelvis up toward him.

Eleanor thought she was prepared for what he was going to do to her, but as it turned out she wasn't.

Henry used both hands to spread her folds before he leaned in and licked her from stern to bough, making her cry out with how good it felt. Then his lips fastened around her clit and sucked the small peak into his mouth. Two fingers pushed inside her, and he increased the suction on her clit, causing her ass to lift off the bed at the intensity of the sensations.

She fisted her hands in the sheets to hold on when he added a third digit, and the pressure inside her increased until her thighs shook with how close she was. When he released the suction on her clit, she whined in desperation, but she should have known better than to think he would let her down.

Teeth clamped down on her swollen nub and nothing had ever felt so good. Her orgasm slammed into her, and she screamed as pleasure rocked through her like a magnitude 9 earthquake.

Tendrils of pleasure were still licking through her body when Henry's cock nudged her entrance before pushing slowly inside, filling her inch by glorious inch. "Are you ready to become mine?"

She nodded, unable to form words when all she wanted to do was feel. Henry's girth was stretching her almost to the point of pain, but the pleasure of being filled far surpassed the burn.

Henry suddenly stopped, and she blinked her eyes open to see him staring down at her with concern lining his face. "Am I hurting you?" He studied her face like he was uncertain what to do next.

Shaking her head, she smiled up at him.

His hands were placed next to her shoulders, supporting his upper body while his hips were nestled between her thighs.

"No. I just need to get used to your size. You're big, but not too big. Please keep going. I want you to fill me completely." She tilted her pelvis and pushed against him, causing his thick shaft to sink into her another inch.

A shudder ran through Henry's body, and he let out a growl. "Fuck, you feel so good. I'm afraid this might be over embarrassingly quick, but I promise I'll make it up to you later. Everything inside me is telling me to hurry up and claim you."

Warmth spread through her chest at his words. He had just given her the best orgasm of her life, and he was apologizing for possibly not lasting long enough to give her another one right away. "Fuck me, baby, and don't worry. I want to feel your body tense when you come inside me."

CHAPTER 45

Henry

Henry's breathing hitched at her words. He was so close to release already there was little chance of him being able to give Eleanor another orgasm before he spilled his seed. But at least he would be able to fulfill her request to come inside her.

Holding his breath, he pulled out a little before pushing back inside her tight sheath. His shaft was so hard it might as well have been made of stone, and his balls were pulled up tight between his legs.

Eleanor lifted her head and stared at where they were connected. Her eyes were glowing, and her fangs were on full display, and he could hardly wait to have her teeth sink into him again. It was a feeling he was quickly getting addicted to.

The next thing he knew he was on his back with Eleanor straddling his hips. A mewl sounded from between her lips as she lowered herself onto his cock until he was buried to the hilt inside her tight, hot body.

"Eleanor." His voice was little more than a growl as he teetered right on the edge of his climax. With her on her back he had nurtured a hope that he would last long enough to bring her with him when he exploded, but with her taking the reins he was left with no control. Particularly when the sight of her on top of him taking control was the most erotic sight he had ever seen.

He wasn't left completely without means, though. Lowering his gaze to her black curls, he reached between her thighs and slid his thumb over her clit. Concentrating on the pleasure button between her legs might help him hold off his own pleasure for a little while longer.

"Henry." Her hands were on his chest when she slowly lifted off him until just the head of his dick was still inside her. "Are you ready to be mine for eternity?" Sultry red eyes met his.

"Yes." He nodded, lifting his gaze to watch the stunning vision of a woman above him.

A wide grin spread across her face before she slammed her body down on his, forcing his cock into her tight pussy, and tearing down the last remnants of his control.

Pleasure flooded his body as his shaft danced a happy dance inside its new favorite place. A few seconds later, Eleanor's pussy clamped down on his cock, and he roared her name as he kept coming inside her.

Instinct made him reach for her and pull her down on top of him before he sank his teeth into her shoulder. Pleasure immediately tore through him, even more intense than before. Then Eleanor's teeth penetrated his skin, and he fell into an ocean of ecstasy so deep he wasn't sure he would ever surface.

His breathing was still ragged when he again became aware of his surroundings. Eleanor was still on top of him, and his arms were wrapped around her.

Henry rolled them slowly onto their sides before he pulled his head back to look at her. The smile on her face was filled with happiness, and her eyes were full of love when they met his. He wanted to tell her how beautiful she was, but his throat clogged with emotion, and he couldn't get a single word out.

"I love you, Henry, my mate." Her hand came up, and her fingertips caressed lightly down his cheek. "You're the most gorgeous man I've ever met and now you're irrevocably mine."

Henry nodded and swallowed hard. "I'm yours, and you're mine." He smoothed his hand down her spine before he let it settle on her hip. "And thank God you are, because I don't think I would've been able to give you up even if you weren't."

EPILOGUE

Henry

Henry hadn't even opened his eyes yet, but the scent that filled his nose made his whole body fill with happiness and desire. Without moving or cracking an eyelid, he let his senses tell him what he wanted to know.

He was on his side with his mate tucked against his front, her body relaxed. Her head was resting on his arm with her hair tickling his chin. His right hand was resting on the curve of her hip, and his hard cock was nestled against the crack of her ass.

He wanted to move, but he knew that as soon as he did, they would be all over each other. And as much as he couldn't wait to make love to his mate again, he wanted to take a moment to just enjoy the knowledge that he had found his true mate, and she was more extraordinary than he had ever expected. They were perfect for each other but not in the muted comfortable way he had expected. Their relationship was hungry, fierce, and wild compared to what he had thought it would be. And he loved it.

Henry slowly opened his eyes and took in his surroundings. He had no idea how many hours had passed since they'd arrived at the farmhouse, but there was still no light visible at the edges of the thick blinds, so the day had yet to begin.

The beautiful woman in his arms stirred, and her ass pressed more firmly against his shaft. It was all it took to ignite the simmering desire in his body and turn it into a burning need.

He had lost count of how many times they had made love before they fell into an exhausted stupor. But it wasn't enough, and he suspected it never would be. Whatever happened in their lives, he would always crave her touch, her words, and her loving presence.

Pulling in a deep breath to fill his lungs with her delicious scent, he slid his hand from her hip, across her belly and down between her thighs. She moaned when his middle finger grazed her clit before sliding through her soft moist folds. He dipped his finger inside her before pulling it back out to circle her sensitive nub.

"Henry." His name was little more than a breath passing her lips.

A smile spread across his face, and he leaned in and kissed the soft skin directly below her earlobe.

Eleanor let out another moan and wriggled her ass against him. "Please make love to me. I want to feel your pleasure again. You should've warned me I would be able to feel your climax. I thought I might be going crazy and was imagining things."

Henry chuckled. "I didn't expect it to take effect so soon, and to be honest I wasn't sure it would happen at all since you're not a shifter. But I realize now that feeling each other's feelings has nothing to do with species and everything to do with the true mate bond."

Her hand suddenly grabbed his thigh before she ground her ass more firmly against his swollen shaft. "I've concluded that I like shifter bonds better than vampire bonds. But it's going to be a struggle to stay away from you long enough to do anything other than this."

He sucked in a breath. It was hard to think of much else than sex with her soft ass threatening to cause his brain to short-circuit with lust. "We'll…get used to it." *Maybe.* He wasn't sure he ever would. But then only a few hours had passed since they mated. He was still adjusting to what having a mate was like.

Henry moved down a little before nudging her opening with his cock. "Are you ready for me, beautiful?"

Eleanor's chuckle was low and sultry. "I don't think there will ever come a time when I'm not."

He kissed her shoulder and pushed into her slowly. The urgency he had felt before they mated had faded a little, but that didn't mean he was less eager to fill her and hear her moans of pleasure. She had fast become the most important person in his life, and that was how it would stay for as long as they walked the earth, and considering they were immortal that might end up being an extremely long time.

Henry thrust into her using long slow strokes, determined to take his time. Using his middle finger, he circled her clit slowly and measuredly, paying attention to her breathing and the tension in her body. He had noticed she breathed like a shifter or human most of the time, but when she was close to coming, she often forgot to pull air into her lungs and her thighs started shaking.

Her grip on his thigh tightened. "Faster. Please." She pushed back against him in an obvious attempt to make him comply.

He chuckled. "No, this time will be slow. We have already fucked hard and fast several times. A little variety won't hurt."

Eleanor let out a small impatient whine. "You're going to drive me crazy. I'm not a very patient person."

Henry laughed. "All the more reason to practice pacing yourself. And I'll be happy to help." At least for as long as his patience lasted. His balls were already pulled up tight, and he knew he wouldn't last much longer.

"Is that so?" Her voice was filled with mischief. And that was all the warning he got before she grabbed the hand he had between her legs and pulled it up to her mouth. Her teeth slid into his wrist, and he jerked with the spike of pleasure that shot directly to his cock.

His plan for taking this slow was immediately overpowered by the need that took hold of his body, causing him to growl and pound into her with a desperation that rivaled the frenzy of mating.

Eleanor tensed, and her body clamped down on his dick when she came, her cry of pleasure muffled against his wrist. And he followed a few seconds later, growling as he filled her with his cum.

Henry let his breathing settle before he pulled out and rolled onto his back. "Those fangs of yours are lethal. Whenever you bite me, I lose control. You have an unfair advantage, you know? How am I ever going to be able to say no to you?"

Chuckling, Eleanor rolled toward him before snuggling against his side and placing a hand on his chest. "Do you want to say no to me?"

Henry looked down into his mate's beautiful brown eyes. "No. And even if I did, I don't think I would've been able to. You have me firmly in your pocket, beautiful."

"Or by the balls." She reached between his legs and gently cupped his balls.

Henry groaned as his cock twitched, blood already heading south to fill the appendage again. "True."

∞∞∞

Gawen

Gawen stared at the ceiling of the room he was in. It was a small sitting room with a couch that was far from long enough to fit his tall frame. But he had insisted that Nes stay in the living room with the bigger couch to ensure she was comfortable.

But it wasn't the couch he was on that was keeping him awake. It was the stunning woman in the room next to his. The knowledge that there was only a door separating them was enough to have his body revved up and ready to go, and it had already stayed like that for hours.

His dick was hard, and his balls were aching from the need for release, but he didn't feel comfortable jerking off with Nes so close. For some reason it felt wrong, even though there was no reason why she would ever find out.

A muffled cry made him tense, and he held his breath to listen. But when a minute went by without another sound, he pulled in a deep breath and relaxed his muscles.

There had been sounds of the couples enjoying themselves for more than an hour after everyone had found their rooms, but for the last few hours everything had been quiet. But with dawn fast approaching, he wasn't sure how much longer it would last. Someone would get up soon, considering they needed to leave early to locate Amber.

A whine that ended in a gasp made him sit up. The sound had come from the living room where Nes was sleeping. But he was loath to go in there to check on her when he didn't know why she had made those sounds. She could be...

Gawen swallowed hard to try to get the image he had conjured of a very naked Nes pleasuring herself out of his mind. But it was impossible when it was something he would give a lot to witness. With her consent of course.

More blood filled his already hard cock and with a groan he gave up his fight not to touch himself. Reaching into his boxers, he wrapped his hand around his thick shaft and gave it a tug. His whole body stiffened with how good it felt to finally give in to his need for release.

Conscious of his responsibility not to ruin the furniture, he silently slid off the couch. After glancing at the door to make sure it was still closed, he pushed his boxers down to midthigh before he sat down on his heels.

Gawen spit in his hand before he coated his straining cock with the liquid. Shuddering with the pent-up need that had been present since he first laid eyes on the beautiful wolf, he silently berated himself for jerking off with an unlocked door between them. But he couldn't stop himself anymore. He needed release to be able to rest and try to keep pretending that Nes didn't really affect him.

Closing his eyes, he let his desire consume him. He tightened his grip around his thick shaft and pumped his fist faster and faster while biting the inside of his cheek so as not to growl with the mounting pleasure.

He was just on the cusp of coming when something made him open his eyes. He couldn't remember hearing anything, but as soon as he opened his eyes, his gaze landed on Nes.

She was standing in the doorway completely still with her eyes locked on his middle. Her hair was messier than before, and her eyes were wide, and all he could think was how she looked even more stunning than before.

Pleasure tore through him, and his dick pulsed with his release. The growl that rumbled low in his throat was raw and hungry. And the object of his hunger was staring at him with an open mouth as his cum splattered on the floor at her feet.

***

Nes

Nes should leave. She should turn around and close the door behind her and leave the gorgeous man alone while he was pleasuring himself.

But her feet wouldn't move. They were frozen to the floor. And her stare was locked on Gawen's massive cock jerking with his climax. She had never watched anything so erotic in her life and it was impossible to look away. And the deep growl rumbling in his chest was only making the whole scene more enticing.

Letting her eyes glide over his bunched abs and hard chest, she started when her eyes met his glowing blue ones. She had noticed his beautiful, soulful eyes with a hint of sadness the first time she laid eyes on him, but now they were utterly mesmerizing.

"Nes."

The sound of her name passing his lips while his hand was still wrapped around his shaft made her gasp and snap out of her frozen state. Heat spread up her neck to her face, and she hastily took a step back and closed the door between them.

Her heart was racing in her chest when she hurried out of the house. She couldn't stay there and wait for him to come ask her why she had entered his room without knocking. It was unforgivable to invade someone's privacy like that, and in her flustered haste to leave, she hadn't even apologized. She shuddered to think what he must think of her.

Nes leaned against the side of her car, facing away from the house before sliding down to land on her ass on the ground.

She had a tendency to be skeptical of new people, but that was no excuse for how she had treated Gawen since she'd met him. Kneeing him in the nuts and watching him masturbate. And all within a few hours of meeting him. What would be next? Would she accidentally trip and fall on his dick, and thereby end up raping the poor guy?

She shivered at the image that thought produced in her mind. Riding Gawen's thick cock while staring into his amazing glowing eyes. That was a scenario that would be featured in her fantasies for a long time to come.

Nes let out a deep sigh. *Get a grip, you stupid bitch. He's not for you. You're not worthy of someone like him.*

---THE END---

BOOKS BY CAROLINE S. HILLIARD

Highland Shifters

A Wolf's Unlikely Mate, Book 1
Taken by the Cat, Book 2
Wolf Mate Surprise, Book 3
Seduced by the Monster, Book 4
Tempted by the Wolf, Book 5
Pursued by the Panther, Book 6
True to the Wolf, Book 7
Mated to the Myth, Book 8

Troll Guardians

Captured by the Troll, Book 1
Saving the Troll, Book 2
Book 3 – TBA

Elemental Enforcers

Fire in My Blood, Book 1 – February 2024
Book 2 – TBA

ABOUT THE AUTHOR

Thank you for reading my book. I hope the story gave you an enjoyable little break from everyday life.

I write because I love immersing myself in different worlds where I get to set the rules for what is possible and not. The rules may change from series to series, but there is one rule I will never break. There will always be a HEA (happily ever after) for the couples in my stories.

The characters I create tend to take on a life of their own and push the story in the direction they want, which means my stories don't follow a set structure or specific literary style. But so far, the central theme has been romance, and I don't expect that to change anytime soon.

I hope to spend as much time as possible writing in the years to come. Because the real world is so much better with the added adventure and spice of imagination.

You can find me here:
caroline.s.hilliard@gmail.com
www.carolineshilliard.com
www.facebook.com/Author.CarolineS.Hilliard/
www.amazon.com/author/carolineshilliard/
www.goodreads.com/author/show/22044909.Caroline_S_Hilliard

Printed in Great Britain
by Amazon